DRAWN TO MURDER

JJ SULLIVAN

BATTERTON POLICE BOOK 1

OTHER BOOKS BY THIS AUTHOR

As John Lynch (Contemporary Fiction)
The Making of Billy McErlane

Sharon Wright: Butterfly

Darkness Comes

As RJ Lynch (Historical Fiction)
A Just and Upright Man

Poor Law

Cover designed by Jessica Bell Design

This book is a work of fiction. Names, characters, places, and incidents either are products of the author's imagination or are used fictitiously. Any resemblance to actual persons, living or dead, events, or locales is entirely coincidental.

Printed in the United Kingdom

First Printing: November 2021
Mandrill Press

978-1-910194-30-0

PROLOGUE

They'd taken Saville's watch and phone when they left and he had no idea what time it was. Or even what day – had he passed a night here? More than one? He didn't know. He did know he'd wet himself when he could hold on no longer and that made him even more uncomfortable than he would have been in any case. He was as stiff as a board, he was angry, and he was lonely – but, most of all, he was afraid. He wanted to believe this must be a mistake, that no-one disliked him enough to do this deliberately. And it was almost possible. But not quite. Without Rita, it might have been. But there was no point in thinking about "without Rita," because it was pursuit of Rita that had brought him here.

He'd seen the dark blue Renault too many times to think it was coincidence. Sometimes she'd be behind him, sometimes coming the other way. Sometimes she'd be parked by the side of the road. But she always made sure he saw her and knew she was watching him.

At first, he told himself he was mistaken. It had been a long time ago and Rita hadn't been a woman then. She'd been a girl. It took a while before he could even remember her name. But he did remember what they'd done to her. It was something he'd never done since, something he could scarcely believe he'd done even that once.

Just thinking about it caused him shame.

He hadn't seen Rita since that day, which meant for twenty years, give or take. But she was back, and she was stalking him. And so, in the end, he'd decided it was an opportunity. A chance to do what he should have done twenty years ago. To apologise. To say he was sorry. That he couldn't believe he'd joined in with the others. Yes, hormones were hormones, adrenaline was adrenaline, testosterone was testosterone – but none of that excused them. Nothing could. And perhaps her reappearance in his life was an opportunity sent by God or whatever fate you believed in to make amends. So he set off in pursuit.

The roads she'd chosen should have been a warning. They got narrower and narrower; the sort of road of which a rally driving friend had once said, 'What stops me giving it full welly is the thought that there might be someone as daft as me coming the other way.' He had found himself hoping that there was, because that would bring her to a halt and he'd be able to get out of the car, walk up to her, say he was sorry and ask her forgiveness. But it didn't happen and he realised that, in the gathering dark, someone coming the other way would have clocked her headlights.

So he kept going, until it became clear that they'd left the road and were now on a canal towpath. He knew at that point he should forget the whole thing, back up and drive away, but that decision was taken from him because the Renault stopped, right by a building that he supposed had once been a lock keeper's home, and a Land Rover pulled out from the side of the building and stopped behind him.

Seconds later, the Land Rover's driver was opening his car door and pointing something at him. The next thing he knew, he'd been here, trussed up like this.

He'd thought about that thing the man had pointed at him, the shock he'd felt and the effect it had on him and he assumed it must have been a taser. He was pretty sure, though, that he wasn't dealing with cops. Could you buy tasers if you weren't official? He supposed you could buy anything if you had the money and knew where to ask.

Since then he'd been here, with nothing to drink and nothing to eat. He'd shouted until he was hoarse, but that had been a waste of time. He might as well have saved his breath. Except for the snuffling. He'd given up on attracting human attention, but from time to time there were sounds of animals close by. Rats? Something bigger? Whenever he'd heard them, he'd kicked out his feet and shouted. Anything to keep whatever it was away. But what if he fell asleep? He might have been left here to die, alone, of thirst and starvation. A horrible way to go. But to be eaten? By something he couldn't see? Fear rose in his throat.

3

CHAPTER 1

It had happened twenty years ago; for Jamie Pearson, it might as well have been yesterday. He'd gone to the recreation ground hoping to see Rita – hoping that, this time, he'd get up the courage to speak to her. Tell her how he felt. Ask her out. He didn't have much money, but so what? Rita wasn't used to a lot of money either. And he didn't want to go to expensive places with her – just to be in her company. Hear her voice. See that wonderful smile.

And she had been there. And Jamie had failed. Completely. Not just to speak to her – to come to her aid. Okay, the young men who wrestled her to the ground, who lifted her skirt, who ripped her pants in their urgency to be on top of her, to be inside her – they were older than he was, and bigger, and stronger, and better fighters. But there were times when you had to do what you had to do, whatever the price you'd have to pay. And this was one of those times. He'd known that then; he knew it now. And, just maybe, some of the other kids might have joined in on his side.

That would have been even better than getting up the courage to speak to her. If he'd done that, she'd have known how he felt.

But he hadn't. He hadn't stayed to watch – at least that couldn't be held against him. He'd left. An act of abject cowardice for which, twenty years later, he still couldn't forgive himself.

That was why he'd joined the police. Life as a cop was a continuous search for the opportunity to help someone who needed it. That wasn't true for everyone in the force and he didn't kid himself it was, but that's how it was for Jamie. An endless, day in day out hunt for the chance to make up for his failure as a sixteen-year-old youth.

It never occurred to him to wonder, if it felt like yesterday to him, how must it feel to Rita?

Perhaps it should have.

* * *

A missing adult was not in itself the business of the Major Crime Investigation Team, and two uniformed police constables were sent to investigate. DI Susanna David was just wondering whether she had time to get to the high street and look for a new dress when they radioed in to tell their sergeant what they had found. Detective Superintendent McAvoy was taking Susanna to a wedding two weeks from now. She'd be meeting his family for the first time since she and Chris had become an item and she wanted to make an impression. And how was she going to squeeze in a visit to the hairdresser? Then she took the Control Room's call and thoughts of dresses and hairdressers faded away. She said, 'They're sure the death is suspicious? Yes, of course they are – you wouldn't have called me otherwise.'

'No, ma'am. SOCO are on their way.'

'Well done, Ronnie. I'll get a team together and we'll join them.'

She stepped into the MCIT office. The only Detective Sergeant available was Rayyan Padgett and Nicola Hayward was the only Detective Constable, so choosing her team was easy. It was also fine – if she'd been able to choose from the whole of MCIT, she might very well have picked these two. They were both still in their twenties so their keenness had not been blunted, they were committed and they had brains – not something she could say of every detective she'd worked with. If she had anything against them at all it was that Nicola's tall, slender grace made Susanna, five feet six herself but on the cusp of forty and acquiring a little weight she felt she'd be better without, feel shabby. But that was no way to choose someone for your team. A Detective Inspector who feared competition from one of her constables should probably be looking for another job.

She told them what had happened. 'It's early days. There are limits to what we can do until SOCO are finished, but that will take a while and I don't want the body sent to the mortuary until I've seen it in situ. So let's take a look at the house and maybe find a neighbour or two to talk to.'

Nicola said, 'Do we know who it is?'

'The house belongs to Terence Carpenter. Is the body also his? We'll soon know.'

'Carpenter?' said Rayyan. 'You mean…'

6

'Yes,' said Susanna. 'Terence Carpenter, lawyer. Partner in Carpenter and Carpenter. I've crossed swords with him and I'm sure you have, too.'

* * *

36 Parkside Ave reflected just how much financial success Carpenter and Carpenter were enjoying. It was set well back from the road, large gardens front and back were in excellent condition, and the house was beautifully maintained. A dark red Aston Martin sat in the driveway. If this had been in most parts of town, the crime scene tape across the gate would have brought a small crowd of people out onto the pavement, eager to know what was going on. People who lived in Parkside Avenue didn't gawp like that. They'd have thought it common. The three cops were, though, aware of faces looking out from upstairs windows in more than one house. A constable was at the tape in case anyone tried to pass it. Susanna said, 'PC Pearson, isn't it? Jamie?'

'Yes, ma'am.'

'You were one of those who found the body?'

'Yes, ma'am.'

'How did you come to be here?'

'Ma'am, his office rang to say they hadn't seen Mr Carpenter for several days. He didn't answer his phone and he didn't come to the door when his secretary rang the bell. They became disturbed enough to ask us to break in.'

'Several days? How long precisely?'

'Today is Friday, ma'am. It's one week today since Mr Carpenter was last seen at work. There was the weekend, of course, but...'

'But he'd been missing all week. Understood. So you broke in?'

'Neither the partner nor the secretary had a key. We asked a neighbour, who told us if he had offered her a key she'd have refused to take it."

'Interesting,' said Susanna. 'And Carpenter lives alone? Or lived, if it turns out to be his body in there?'

'It is his body, ma'am. I've seen him often enough in the custody suite. And, yes, he lived alone.'

'And you found the death suspicious? Did you declare life extinct yourself?'

'Yes, ma'am. There was no need to call a paramedic. He'd been dead long enough not to smell too good. He was naked on his bed. There are no restraints there now, but his wrists are chafed as though he'd been struggling to escape from something that was holding him down.'

Rayyan handed out protective paper suits and overshoes. As they were suiting up prior to entering the house, Susanna said to Jamie Pearson, 'You've done well.' She turned and stepped cautiously past him, the others following. They climbed the stairs in order of seniority, taking care to stand only on the stepping plates the SOCOs had laid for that purpose. When they reached the master bedroom, they found the crime scene manager in the same protective gear going through a chest of drawers and picking over the items in it one by one. One of his officers was swabbing for DNA. Susanna was aware that Nicola was watching her closely, and she remembered doing the same on her first few murder enquiries. She also remembered not wanting to ask why the DI did what he did for fear of being in the way. What she knew now was that her job was to help those below her to become better detectives.

She said, 'Nic, there are various questions we ask ourselves at this point. The obvious ones are, Why this person? Why here? Why now? And those are the things we're going to be probing over the next – well, however long it takes. But there are other questions we need to address, and they come up the first time we arrive at the scene. Who was here at the time of death? What happened? Why did it happen? You won't find the answers by looking around. But remembering what you saw can ring bells later when the evidence starts to build.' She inclined her head towards the crime scene manager. 'That, of course, is why even Charlie here won't have set foot in this room until his photographer was satisfied he had a pictorial record of everything. And we can refer back to that record whenever we need to.' To the crime scene manager, she said, 'Are we going to be in the way?'

The CSM sighed. 'It could be a month before

we finish. Unless you can stay away that long, you'll always be in the way. But of course you can't. Whoever was here was very careful.' He waved his head towards the landing. 'There's a Dyson out there; if you can believe this, it looks as though the killer vacuumed the carpet when he was done. And then took the drum away with him.'

'Charlie, I know it's early doors, but…'

'But you'd like to know what I can tell you so far. Well, we think something was used to secure the man's wrists and removed after he was dead. But take a look at his stomach.'

Susanna leaned in close and then recoiled. 'Semen?'

'It looks as though one of the last things he did before he went to meet his maker was to ejaculate. And as in my opinion his wrists were shackled to the bed frame at the time…'

'Someone helped him,' said Nicola.

'Charming,' said Rayyan. 'I wonder if they thought they were doing him a favour.'

'I'm going back to the station,' said Susanna. 'There's nothing I can do until we know what the post-mortem says. I'll ring Professor Baines and see when he can do that. I need to find out who's going to be Senior Investigating Officer, and get someone to set up an incident room and log the case on HOLMES. Rayyan, you and Nicola go door-to-door. I don't suppose anyone saw anything, but you never know. Find out what

Carpenter's neighbours thought of him. We know what he was like as a lawyer, but what sort of man was he outside work? Do each house together – one of you to ask the questions and one to hear the things people don't say. Start with the woman who said she wouldn't take his key if he offered it to her. I'll get someone else to notify Carpenter and Carpenter. It's common courtesy, it needs to be done, and I'd like to know what they have to say about him.'

Rayyan said, 'Ma'am, are we working on the assumption that this was a sex transaction that went wrong?'

'That's one possibility. But maybe that's just what we are meant to think. And even if it was, what kind of sex transaction? Was it with a woman or another man? Was it a romantic interlude or did money change hands? Was Carpenter tied up against his will or because that was how he liked it? An open mind, Rayyan. More cases have been buggered up by coppers making assumptions than by anything else. We don't even know for certain who that semen belongs to. It might be his, and it might belong to whoever killed him. We won't be sure until we get the DNA results, and God knows how long that's going to take. What do you make of the garden?'

'It's very well-tended,' said Nicola, who was used to the DI's sudden changes of direction.

'It is indeed, And the lawn?'

'You could play billiards on it,' said Rayyan.

'Which tells us…?'

'I can't see Carpenter looking after it like that when he got home from a day making our life difficult. So there's a gardener.'

'There's a gardener. And he's been here this week. At this time of year, grass grows faster than the Chief Constable's moustache.'

Rayyan smiled. The chief's objections to facial hair were well known and any male officer who hoped to progress in the force was clean-shaven – but the chief constable was a woman and so the strictures did not apply to her.

'So we need to find the gardener,' said Susanna. 'When was he last here and what did he see?'

'Or she,' said Rayyan.

Susanna eyed him with a smile that wasn't entirely affectionate. 'Rayyan. Just between us, and while no-one else is listening, can we take the gender equality business as read? When I say, "he," I mean, "he or she." Except when I don't. And I expect you to know the difference.'

Nicola gave Rayyan a sympathetic glance. When the inspector told you off, it was best to pretend it hadn't happened.

CHAPTER 2

The crime scene manager arranged to have the body shipped to the morgue where Professor Baines, who was in a hurry, started on the post-mortem so quickly that Susanna missed the beginning. He then left for a weekend of golf and a family dinner but, for the major crime team, work was just beginning. Baines may have been eager to start his weekend, but he was never less than totally committed, and the post-mortem took more than four hours. By the time Susanna got back to the station, the afternoon was well advanced. Detective Superintendent McAvoy was in overall charge of Major Crime, but too senior to be SIO on any particular case less important than the murder of a prime minister. For Susanna, that was both a bonus and a problem. She said, 'You know how much time a case like this takes. You should – you did enough of them before you made Superintendent. I don't think we'll see much of each other this weekend. I was really looking forward to your cooking, but it isn't going to happen now.'

'It's cassoulet, Suze. And cassoulet only improves with time. I'll put it in the freezer.'

'It'll be something to look forward to. If I'm lucky, and if you're still awake, I'll be done here in time to get there for a cuddle before bedtime. If it's too late, I'll go straight home.'

'I shall be waiting with open arms whenever you are able to make it.'

She didn't attempt to kiss him. The blinds were down on his windows, but that didn't mean they couldn't be seen. She joined the team in the incident room, marvelling as she always did at how the smooth-running machine that was a major crime team slipped into action. This was by no means the only case they had on their hands, but everything was happening as it should.

The coroner had been advised, maintaining the legal fiction that he was the person in charge. He would open an inquest and adjourn it until the police were able to provide information on which he could recommend a verdict to his jury. The local press, radio and TV station had received a release telling them that Terence Carpenter, lawyer, had suffered a suspicious death and inviting anyone with information, however seemingly insignificant, to share it with the police – anonymously, if necessary. Marion Trimble, a civilian member of the team and the designated HOLMES receiver, was at her keyboard ready to enter everything into the computer system that had taken the place of old-fashioned murder books. Half a dozen officers, DCs and DSs, were at their desks and each knew their role in this enquiry. They also knew that private time was going to be at a severe premium until the back of this enquiry was broken. Nicola had already pinned to a whiteboard a photograph of the body taken by the

SOCO photographer in his home as well as photos of the scene and Susanna handed her two more from the post-mortem. Someone had arranged tea and coffee and a large box of chocolate doughnuts sat on a table.

Susanna said, 'We'll start with what we know. DCI Blazeley has been appointed SIO. He's in court right now on another case entirely; he'll be joining us later. The house had not been ransacked and there were no signs that anything had been stolen. There is a safe. It's in a wardrobe in a spare bedroom and it's opened with a combination. Carpenter's visitor might have opened it and might not – we don't know. Nor do we as yet know what's in it; I've asked for a locksmith to open it for us.'

Nicola said, 'Have you asked Carpenter's partner whether he knows the combination?'

'If I ask him, he may want to be present when the safe is opened. Obviously, I can refuse easily enough – the house is a crime scene. But that's a thought.' She turned to Gareth Forester. Forester was in his forties and had been a detective constable for more than fifteen years. He'd never applied for promotion because he was one of the major crime team's specialist interviewers and he loved that work so much he didn't want to give it up just for a higher salary and the right to call himself a detective sergeant. His empathetic manner, though, made him a perfect choice to give bad news to people and, when she learned that he had no interview scheduled until later that day, Susanna had asked him to go to Carpenter and Carpenter. 'Gareth, we'll hear about your visit to Carpenter's partner in a few minutes but, for now, did he mention a safe in Carpenter's house?'

Forester shook his head. 'Not a word.'

'Hmm. Perhaps he was too grief stricken to think about it.'

A smile passed across Forester's face. 'If he was grieving, he kept it well hidden.'

'Interesting. Perhaps he doesn't know it's there. Which might make what's in there more interesting.'

Rayyan said, 'Or it might just be empty.'

'Thank you, Rayyan – I don't know what I'd do without you to puncture my balloon. Now: the post-mortem. It will be days, at the very least, before we find out most of what Professor Baines will have to tell us, but I'll give you the immediate headlines. Carpenter has been dead for at least a few days, so whoever was with him when he died has had lots of time to bury any evidence and make themselves scarce. Carpenter's wrists had been restrained. Professor Baines won't commit himself but he thinks it was with cable ties. If so, they've been taken away. Death was caused by asphyxiation and the Professor believes that a plastic bag was most likely used. Once again, SOCO found no such bag. Carpenter had been masturbated to orgasm immediately before – or, indeed, at the point of – death; there had been no anal intrusion.'

Nicola said, 'Do we know that for sure? Aren't there drugs that can relax the sphincter?'

'Professor Baines thinks we can be sure, yes. He says whatever drugs might have been used, and it will be days at the very least before we have a toxicology report, there would still be signs that something had been in there. He found none.'

Rayyan said, 'If there had been, we might be able to tell what had done the intruding. In which case, we might know whether the killer was a man or a woman. As it is…'

'I wonder,' said Susanna, 'whether we might hold off for a while on using that word "killer." There is no evidence as yet that Carpenter was murdered. It's well established that reducing the flow of oxygen during sexual congress can heighten the pleasure. People have died while masturbating after they've hung themselves from the ceiling and accidentally kicked away whatever they were standing on. We have no way of knowing at this point whether that's what happened here.'

'But in that case,' said another detective sergeant, 'wouldn't we have expected whoever was with him when he died to call it in? They might not have wanted to hang around or say who they were, but surely they wouldn't have just left the body without telling anyone it was there?'

'And they'd have tried to resuscitate,' said Nicola. 'And if they'd done that, the pathologist

17

would have seen the signs and told us.'

'Both of those things are true,' said Susanna. 'And I agree that murder is the most likely cause of death. But we can't know for certain. Not yet. For the moment, we are looking for someone who left the scene of a suspicious death. We are not certain that we are looking for a killer.'

'No,' said Nicola. 'I bet we are, though.' Several heads in the room nodded in agreement.

Susanna said, 'To return to what we do know, the pathologist confirms that Carpenter had not eaten for several hours. Whatever he did eat had deteriorated to the point where identifying it was difficult. He thinks, though, that it was probably a tuna salad sandwich. I assume that that was his lunch, but forensics found no empty tins of tuna in the recycling boxes. The dishwasher was full of clean dishes but there was no lettuce and no tomatoes in the fridge. That makes it possible the sandwich was something he bought to eat at work, which could pinpoint Friday as the day he died because that was his last day in the office. Please check that. Carpenter had, however, drunk whisky very shortly before death. We know that because the reek of whisky when he was opened up was unmistakable. And what is interesting about that is that, once again, forensics found no used glasses anywhere in the house. Carpenter had a number of Glencairn whisky glasses – that's a particular shape valued by whisky drinkers if you're not familiar with it – but all were clean and put away.

The same goes for some very nice heavy crystal glasses. Carpenter was clearly a man of taste, at least in his personal goods, and saw no need to stint. Now. What did you learn from the neighbours?'

CHAPTER 3

The door-to-door interviews had produced mixed results. No-one had seen Carpenter come home, but two people had seen him driven away from the house in a taxi at about seven the previous Friday evening. When Susanna heard that she said, 'Excellent. Chances are he returned the same way.' She turned to Marion Trimble. 'Two new actions: Find the taxi driver who picked him up from home and find the one who took him back there. Where was he dropped off, where was he picked up, and was anyone with him?'

Rayyan said, 'Ma'am, we don't know for sure that that was the day he died.'

'No, we don't. But we do know it was the last time he was seen, so we'll work on the basis that he died last Friday until we have evidence to the contrary. What else did the door-to-door tell us?'

Rayyan and Nicola had called on the neighbour who said she had nothing to do with Carpenter if she could avoid it. Rayyan had had to school himself to deal with witnesses like Victoria Carew; though she must be in her fifties, she had the same sort of grace as Nicola Hayward and was every bit as tall but she had that self-assured air that only came from having been born into money. Rayyan struggled with a combination of feelings. On the one hand, he was slightly intimidated by the evidence that this woman moved in a world that was not the one he was used to. His parents had been well off, his father a respected academic, but they'd avoided social occasions whenever they could. On the other hand, he could not quite prevent himself from wondering how different a person Victoria Carew might become when naked and between the bedsheets. It did not help that he could see Nicola out of the corner of his eye and her smirk suggested she had a good idea of what was going on in his head. He said, 'You told the officer that you would not have accepted a key if Mr Carpenter offered it.'

'He was not a nice person. I say "was" because I'm assuming from the level of your interest that he is dead and that you think someone killed him.'

'We can't confirm that at this point,' said Rayyan.

'I think you just did. Well, I shall not mourn his passing and I shall hope that whoever buys that house is an altogether nicer person. I have never agreed with the sentimental nonsense that one should not speak ill of the dead. Terence Carpenter was an out and out shit. I expect you'd like to know in what his shittiness consisted?'

'If you can bring yourself to tell us,' said Nicola.

'It will be a pleasure. In the first place, he treated his wife abysmally.'

'Wife?' said Nicola. 'There's been no…'

'No mention of a wife. There wouldn't be. They married nearly thirty years ago. It was a sham from the very beginning. She didn't divorce him until seven years after they were married, and she did that only when she found a proper man to marry, but I don't believe they lived together for more than a few weeks. And, in fact, she didn't divorce him at all – the marriage was annulled because it had never been consummated.'

Rayyan said, 'You seem to know a great deal about this, Mrs Carew.'

'Ms. Ms Carew. I know so much about it because the woman he married was my sister.'

'I see,' said Rayyan. 'We'll need to speak to her. Could you give me her current name and address, please?'

Carew picked up an address book from the mantelpiece, turned the pages and held the book out to Nicola. 'Jenny McMurtry. My sister. If you contact her, please bear in mind that she now has a husband and children.'

'We'll exercise discretion,' said Nicola, entering the details into her tablet. 'I see she lives not far from here. When did you last see her?'

'Last Saturday. We meet in town every Saturday to have lunch and go round the shops. She won't come here because she's afraid of running into him. Though I suppose that's not something she need worry about any more.'

Rayyan said, 'You said, "in the first place." What else was there you didn't like about him?'

'He was an execrable neighbour. I'm sure you'll hear that from other people, too. If anyone parked in front of his house, he objected. I don't mean across his driveway – I mean anywhere in front of his house. Even though the height of his hedge meant he couldn't see the offending vehicle and even though this road is a public highway. He'd write unpleasant notes and put them under the windscreen wipers. In fact, if you speak to the Wainwrights at number 42, I think you'll find they went to court to get an injunction against him. And he a lawyer! The man had no class at all. I sometimes think it's a shame the days of horse-whipping are gone.'

'Anything else?' asked Rayyan.

'He objected to people burning leaves. In fact, he objected to almost anything other people might be doing. When the daughter of the Mariners at number 25 married and they erected a marquee on their back lawn – their back lawn, mark you, on the other side of the road and invisible from any window in his house – he objected on the grounds that it lowered the tone of the neighbourhood.'

Nicola said, 'I didn't think that was something you could go to court for.'

'He claimed that the size of the marquee meant that they should have had planning permission. Of course, by the time he'd registered that complaint officially the wedding was over, the guests had departed and the company that owned the marquee had dismantled it and taken it back to wherever it came from.' She sniffed. 'I think his real objection was that he had not been invited.'

Nicola smiled. 'Were you?'

'Of course. I make it a point to be on good terms with all of my neighbours. All of them except him.'

'One more point,' said Rayyan, 'and then we'll leave you. Do you know whether Mr Carpenter had a gardener?'

'Indeed he did. He had the same gardener as me. I suppose you'd like his name and address, too?'

'If you'd be so kind.'

* * *

'All very interesting,' said Susanna. 'You'll follow that up with the other neighbours, of course. Marion, put that on HOLMES as an action. Tomorrow or Sunday would be best – a place like that, people will all be home, washing cars and trimming rose bushes. And see what you can find out about Ms Carew. I'm not suggesting she's a suspect – though I'm not suggesting she isn't, either – but living alone in a house that size in such an expensive street? And employing a gardener? Where does the money come from?' She looked at Gareth Forester. 'Did anyone at Carpenter and Carpenter mention an ex-wife?'

Forester shook his head. 'Not a word.'

'Isn't that interesting? Okay; Jenny McMurtry needs a visit, and it won't wait. Rayyan, Nicola – go round there right now. We'll carry on without you. Marion…'

'I know,' said Marion. 'I'm putting it on HOLMES now.'

'Whatever did we do without the computer?' asked Susanna.

'We missed stuff. Or so I'm told,' said Nicola. 'I'll tell you what I found interesting about Ms Carew. She didn't ask how he died.'

'Didn't she?' said Susanna. 'How very unusual. They always ask that.'

'Unless they already know,' said Nicola. 'You met her, Sarge. Would you describe her as the kind of woman who might help a dying man achieve his final orgasm?'

When Rayyan turned bright red, Nicola grinned at Susanna. 'Not in the prime of life, Ms Carew, but still someone a man might find… Unsettling. Isn't that right, Sarge?'

'Don't tease him,' said Susanna. 'The pair of you get off now. Gareth, tell us how you got on at the law firm.'

* * *

A detective constable would normally have expected to be kept waiting at a law practice because that was how lawyers liked it. The relationship between these two branches of the law can be testy. But there was no delay today, and Gareth Forester was shown into Barney Carpenter's office without delay. The receptionist showing him the way said, 'I think he wants to get off home. He's already heard the news – a journalist rang. Can I bring you coffee? Tea? Water?'

'Tea would be wonderful,' said Gareth.

Barney Carpenter came from behind his desk but did not offer to shake his hand. He said, 'I want you to know, officer, that I think it's a poor show when the brother of a murdered man learns of his death from the press instead of from the police.'

At least that made breaking the news easier than it often was. And this Carpenter was also a lawyer, so there was no need to pretend things were other than they were. Gareth said, 'I'm sorry, Mr Carpenter. I got here as quickly as I could. The press must have been very quick off the mark, but they don't have to do the preparatory work that we do.'

Carpenter ushered him towards two sofas on opposite sides of a low table. 'I think we'll be more comfortable here.' Gareth knew that one of the questions he would later be asked would be how much grief the lawyer had shown immediately after learning that his brother was dead in suspicious circumstances. He'd have no difficulty answering that; there was no grief on display at all. He said, 'Mr Carpenter, we've seen your brother in the custody suite many times, but I don't think we've ever seen you there?'

'Terence liked the face-to-face hostility of criminal law. I prefer commercial law. I'm not by nature confrontational; he was. We have another partner who takes care of conveyancing, making people's wills and so on.'

Not only no obvious signs of grief, but Carpenter had immediately begun to speak of his brother in the past tense. Gareth had enough experience of interviewing people who had suffered the sudden loss of a relative or friend to know how unusual that was. He said, 'Speaking of wills, had he made one of his own?'

Carpenter stood without a word and began to riffle through a filing cabinet drawer. He extracted a document and held it out. 'He had, and this is it. I'm the executor, which is why I have that copy.'

Gareth read the single sheet of paper and handed it back. 'Mr Carpenter, your firm has a thriving criminal practice. If he was in charge of that part of your business, how have you managed for the past week in his absence?'

'Oh, Terence didn't handle all the criminal stuff on his own. Cyril Bonser reported to him. And you must know that, because you will have seen Cyril in your interview rooms even more often than you saw my brother. But if I'd been here, we'd have reported him missing a lot earlier. I was laid low by a dreadful attack of summer flu. Cyril got on with the work and, although they tried to let me know Terence wasn't here, my wife refused to pass on the message. She's a very protective woman.'

If Gareth thought this a very convenient dose of summer flu, whatever summer flu was, only a slight raising of his eyebrows conveyed the fact.

He said, 'Tell me about your brother.'

'Of course. What I imagine you'd like to know is whether I think anyone might have had a wish to end my brother's life.'

Gareth nodded. 'It's always useful to know if there are any obvious people of interest.'

'Of course. In the case of Terence, it may well be that there are far too many. Starting, of course, with me.'

'You, sir?'

'Me. You will have wondered who benefited from my brother's death. As you now know, he has left everything to me. And, as I am his executor, I knew that. I'm not naïve enough to think you won't see me as a prime suspect.' He laughed. 'Especially when it becomes clear that I didn't like my brother one little bit.'

'No, sir?'

'Life dealt Terence a bad hand. I understand that. But the fact is that it's possible to understand without being understanding. I didn't like the things my brother did and I didn't like the way he treated other people.'

'Tell me some more about this bad hand life dealt your brother.'

'Terence was older than me. Our father did very well for himself. Before the war, he was little more than a rag and bone man. Then came 1939, there was huge demand for all sorts of recycled materials, and somehow he landed a contract to supply. I don't know how, this was all years before

I was born, but I imagine some civil servant was better off after the deal than he had been before. And so was our father. By 1945, he was in a pretty good state financially. He spent the next twenty years or so building up his empire and then, when he was nearer seventy than sixty, he dumped the wife who'd supported him through the hard years for a much younger model. His new wife gave him Terence, and ten years later she gave him me. He was eighty when I was born, and my mother was thirty-two. I'm sure you get the picture.

'Our father invested all his ambition into Terence. He had lots of money and insisted Terence should go to the kind of school the very wealthy send their children to. It didn't go well; Terence was never short of anything but it didn't take the other boys long to realise that he was not of their class. His father was a barrow boy and – let's be frank – our mother was little more than a tart and all the money to buy Paris fashions couldn't change that. If Terence had had any sporting ability, he might have been accepted, but he and balls were not made for each other. Not that kind of balls, anyway.'

'He was gay?'

'Yes, he was. Though the people he had to mix with at school would have used less kind words. When he left school, he had done well enough academically to get to Oxford – a school like that will do that for you – but he had a chip on his shoulder the size of a house and he never lost it.'

'Did you go to the same school, sir?'

'No, thank God. Our father died when I was seven and our mother remarried about three months later. Her new husband had different views on education. I went to the local state school. Our mother is still alive, by the way, though her second husband, too, is dead. She lives in Spain now with a toy boy from Balham. I've told her Terence is dead, but I'm not sure she really took it in.'

'You're not bitter? About going to a state school?'

'On the contrary, it was the best thing that could have happened to me. I fitted in, I played football in the winter and cricket in the summer, and it wasn't made clear to me every single day of my school life that people looked down on me. I didn't get to Oxford but I did go to Durham and I had a damn good time there.' He looked up at Gareth. 'I found out what it was that made girls so attractive. In my third year, I met the woman who became my wife. We are still married. We have three lovely children. I could afford – not Eton, not Marlborough, but certainly somewhere good – but I didn't. The youngest is now in the local sixth form college; the other two are both at university. I believe all three are balanced human beings.'

'How did they and your wife get along with your brother?'

'They didn't. My wife detested Terence. I don't think any of my children have seen him for many years.'

'You've been very straightforward in identifying yourself as a person of interest, sir – you mentioned there would be others. Can you tell me who they are?'

* * *

'What did he say to that?' said Susanna.

'Well,' said Gareth, 'first of all, he suggested the children of the first Mrs Carpenter. He said she herself was probably dead…'

Susanna nodded in Marion Trimble's direction. 'More actions. Find that family. When we know who and where they are, we'll decide who is to interview them. Though it's hard to see why they would want to kill Carpenter – he wasn't even born when the wife was abandoned, and they are not in his will. Gareth, did Barney Carpenter suggest any other suspects?'

'He suggested any other gay men his brother has had dealings with over the years, but he couldn't help with names. He said his brother kept that side of his life private.'

'Yes. And I don't suppose he felt like asking questions. You weren't able to speak to Cyril Bonser?'

'Well, I was,' said Gareth. 'I know I should have rung in to see if there were any more actions for me, but Barney Carpenter offered to introduce me and…'

'You did the right thing,' said Susanna. 'Well

done. Talking to him after he knew about the death and had had time to let it sink in would have given him time to get a story together. Tell us what he said.'

* * *

Barney Carpenter 's office had been extremely tidy. Cyril Bonser's was much more as Gareth expected a lawyer's office to be. Apart from the same rows of law books and statutes he had seen in Barney's office, there were files and documents on every surface – the desk, the chairs, the floor. Cyril cleared a chair. 'Excuse the mess. I never seem to get time to clear things away.'

Gareth said, 'Mr Bonser. How did you come to be working for Mr Terence Carpenter?'

'The job was advertised. I applied. I came here for interview. Mr Carpenter asked me about my internships up to then and I answered. He offered me the job.'

'Straight away?'

Bonser appeared to be thinking hard about what he was going to say. Then he shrugged. 'Not quite immediately, no. He said he'd like to hold my cock. I suspect you've heard of gaydar, officer. I'd already seen what I needed to know about him, and that was clearly also true in reverse. So I said I kept it in the usual place.'

'Which he interpreted as an invitation?'

'Indeed. He suggested we continue the interview at his home. He drove me there in the predecessor of that lovely red DB11. He had a DB9 at the time. He was fond of Aston Martins. We spent some time in bed, he told me I'd got the job, and I started a week later.'

'How long ago was that, sir?'

'About four years. Yes, four years next month.'

'And have you and Mr Carpenter been in a relationship for all of that period?'

'Good Lord, no! Terence wasn't one for relationships. He'd indicate occasionally that he fancied a shag. But that wasn't often. I had to get my own needs met elsewhere.'

CHAPTER 4

Jenny McMurtry was at home, drinking tea and eating cake with her husband and their two teenage daughters. She made it clear that their visit was not welcome. 'Terence Carpenter was a mistake. A mistake by the universe and a mistake by me. If you've come to tell me he's dead, you're too late; my sister has already given me the news. So, if you'll excuse me, I have things to do that matter more than a dead man who fooled me and fooled the rest of the world as well.'

Rayyan said, 'We'll make it as quick as we can, Mrs McMurtry. But Terence Carpenter was murdered and we have to find out who killed him. If for no other reason, we need to prevent the same person from killing again.'

Mrs McMurtry did not look at all mollified. 'What you mean is that I should allow a feeling of civic responsibility to interrupt family time.'

'We appreciate the sacrifice, but you may know something that turns out to be invaluable. The huge majority of murders are carried out by people close to the victim.'

'Close? Close! I haven't seen the man for years. Decades.'

The eyes of the two daughters had been on stalks during this exchange. Jenny McMurtry's husband said, 'Darling. Take them into the sunroom. Tell them what they want to know.' He turned towards Nicola and Rayyan. 'Would you like me to bring you some tea or coffee?'

Having achieved his aim, Rayyan was ready to be magnanimous. 'Thank you, Mr McMurtry – but nothing for us. And we'll do our best not to keep your wife any longer than necessary.'

* * *

The sunroom was big enough to hold two large sofas, four other chairs and a keyboard. A violin case lay across the keyboard stool. Around the window sills was a collection of potted plants. The room jutted out into a large lawn surrounded by spacious borders that at this time of year were a riot of colour. Rayyan and Nicola sat on one of the sofas and Jenny McMurtry took the other. Rayyan led the conversation. 'Mrs McMurtry. How did you come to meet Terence Carpenter? And when was that?'

'I was fresh out of finishing school in Switzerland. Did you know that there are five thousand seven hundred and fifty-three people on the list of those in line for the British throne? Well, there are. Who, you might ask, gives a toss? The answer to that is: my father. He reckoned that he was seventy-sixth in line to the throne. If seventy-five people died, he would become king. As long as they were the right seventy-five, of course. And that gave him the most absurd ideas about how he should live his life, and how those of us in his family should live ours. His views on educating

35

sons and daughters were at least fifty years out of date, even then. Nevertheless, they were how things were done in our family – my brother was educated at Harrow and Oxford, and I had to make do with learning to be a wife. Ideally to a diplomat or captain of industry. My brother was not the sharpest tool in the box and I don't think anyone including my father doubted that I was brighter than him and could have benefited much more from that sort of education. But I was a girl and my brother was a boy and educating the girls above the boys was not how it should be done in what my father thought of as our circles.'

Nicola realised that Jenny McMurtry would be able to read the sympathy in her face, because she knew it was there – and the sympathy was real. She said, 'Did the same also apply to Ms Carew?'

'It did. Our financial needs were met with trust funds and I can't complain about money, but our intellectual needs were ignored. A woman did not exist for any purpose except to make a man's life easier. It didn't help that our mother saw things in exactly the same way. But I can assure you that that is not how our daughters are being brought up.'

'I see. And Terence Carpenter?'

'Well, that was a disaster, but it was exactly what happens when you raise girls in the way we were raised. Terence Carpenter called on us at home shortly after he graduated. He had known my brother at school and at Oxford and he knew that my father's business interests meant that he made use of legal professionals. Terence had just set up on his own and he hoped to use the fact that he knew my brother to drum up business. And they laughed at him. Ridiculed him. Mocked him. He had learned to speak in the right way, of course, and he knew how to hold a knife and fork and which wine to drink with which course – but he remained the child of his parents. And he had a most unfortunate fawning manner. When he wanted something, that is – he could be a brute if he found himself in a position of power over others. And that is quite apart from the fact that my brother suspected him of proclivities that should have precluded marriage, though he didn't have the grace to pass that on to me. My God, listen to me! One mention of my disastrous marriage to a lawyer and like a lawyer is how I start to speak.'

Rayyan thought he knew what was coming. 'You felt sorry for him?'

'I've come to regard pity as the single most corrosive, most destructive emotion. But, yes, I felt sorry for Terence. And he played on that. I think he really thought that if we were married he would get business from my father. I think he also imagined he was marrying into money that he would be able to use. As I've said, mine was and is in a trust fund. That made me furious at the time, but now I am glad. We were married only three months after we'd first met. Of my family, only my sister was there, and she attended very much against my father's will. The marriage took place in a registry office. And it was a disaster.'

'Your sister says it was never consummated.'

'As my brother knew, and failed to tell me, my husband was what is now called gay. In those days, people like my father and my brother used other words. My father called him a… Well. What's the point? My father is dead and now so is the object of his ridicule. Is that all?'

Nicola said, 'And your sister is correct?'

'Yes, my sister is correct. The marriage was never consummated.'

'But…?'

'That isn't to say he didn't try. And I do believe that Terence was capable of – I'm not going to call it making love – he was capable of completing the act with a woman.'

'But…?' said Nicola again when Mrs McMurtry once more fell into silence.

'But he could only do it with violence. He needed it to be rape. And I'm afraid that I… I may have been brought up to pretend to believe that men were superior, but I was also educated in a school that taught its girls their value. No one was going to have his way with me by force. Not even my husband.'

Rayyan stood. 'Thank you for talking to us. I'm sorry to have interrupted your meal. We may wish to speak to you again.'

'If you do, please make it at a more convenient time.'

At the door, Rayyan said, 'Your present husband. Diplomat? Or captain of industry?'

Jenny McMurtry gave him the sort of glare she might have given to a spider in her hatbox. 'He's a musician. My father would have been appalled. Appalling my father is not why I chose him for my husband, but it is a very pleasant bonus.'

CHAPTER 5

When they were done with Jenny McMurtry, Rayyan called the incident room and spoke to Marion Trimble. 'The taxi office is between here and the station. If no one else has been assigned that action, perhaps you can give it to us.' There was a pause while Marion checked with the DI and then she was back on the line. 'That's approved, Rayyan. Go ahead.'

Afternoon had not shaded into evening, but the taxi company's dispatch room was already busy. Rayyan had long ago learned that irritating people was not the best way to get their help and so he showed no impatience when it took time for one of the two dispatchers to look through the previous Friday's records. He said, 'Don't you have a book to write things down in?'

'A book!' said the dispatcher. 'How delightfully old-fashioned. I can't remember when we last used a book. Everything is online. And there's an audit trail, so no journeys can be hidden. HMRC don't trust taxi firms – I have no idea why. Last Friday… Yes, here it is. A Mr Carpenter from 36 Parkside Ave to Barracuda Street. Pickup was 7 o'clock, and the driver was available again from 7.20 – so that's when he dropped the passenger off. Which makes sense for that journey.'

'Booked in advance?'

'Yes – booked the previous Friday when we

brought him back from Barracuda Street.'

'Was this a regular thing, then?'

The dispatcher scanned back through the records of several weeks. 'Looks like it. Not every Friday, but quite often. If you want to talk to the driver, his name is Tom Finch and he's outside right now having a cigarette.'

'We will,' said Rayyan. 'Before we do, though, can you check whether one of your taxis took him back to Parkside Avenue?'

'That's a bit more difficult, because it wouldn't have been booked unless he always left there at the same time. Which he didn't.' The dispatcher moved his mouse as he went through the records. 'No. Can't see anything. Hold on, though – there is a way to check.' The mouse moved again and a new file appeared on the screen. The dispatcher said, 'Carpenter is a regular. He has an account with us – we bill him once a month. So, if we took him home …. No. However he got home, it wasn't with us. Maybe he had a pickup and the pickup had a car. I take it you know what goes on in Barracuda Street?'

'Yes,' said Nicola. 'We have a very good idea why a gay man would be in Barracuda Street on a Friday evening.'

The dispatcher's face was a picture of innocence. 'Was he a Willy Woofter, then? I didn't know that.'

Rayyan said, 'Look, I don't go looking for work but that was an offensive expression. I'm going to pretend you didn't say it, but I don't want to hear it again.'

'Sorry,' said the dispatcher, though his expression contradicted his words.

'The other dispatcher said, 'If you want to speak to Tom Finch, you'd better do it now – an airport run has just come in and it's his turn. If we give it to someone else, there'll be hell to pay.'

* * *

Tom Finch easily remembered collecting Carpenter the previous week. 'It's usually me that picks him up.'

'Any particular reason?'

Finch shrugged. 'We get on okay. That doesn't always happen, so if one driver has a good relationship with a customer he tends to get that customer's jobs. I'm happy with it – Mr Carpenter is an account customer but he always tips me a quid. Not everyone is that generous. Why are you asking?'

Nicola said, 'You haven't heard, then?'

'Has something happened?'

'Mr Carpenter was murdered. Very possibly last Friday night.'

Finch had turned white. 'I had no idea. It hasn't been on the radio. Is this public knowledge?'

'The press have it now,' said Rayyan.

'Well, bugger me.' From white, his face turned bright red. 'Sorry – that's the last thing I should say in relation to Mr Carpenter. Well! I suppose

42

that's always going to be a risk if you get up to that sort of thing.'

'That sort of thing?' said Nicola.

'His Friday evening fare was always to Barracuda Street. I never took him right to Number 26 – he liked to be dropped at the end of the road. But I knew where he was going, and he knew I knew. I just thought, you know, good luck to him. Each to his own. It's never appealed to me, but if that was what he wanted… Well, bugger me,' he said again.

Nicola said, 'Number 26?'

'You're not going to play the innocent, are you? Don't tell me the police don't know what kind of people go to Number 26.'

* * *

'Okay,' said Susanna David when they were once more in the incident room. 'We know Carpenter got home because he died there. The question is, how? And the obvious place to find out is Number 26. Marion, have you got a suitable action for these two?'

'Someone needs to talk to the gardener.'

'There you are,' said Susanna. 'The gardener. Off you go.'

'You don't want us to go to Number 26?'

'No, I don't. I have a better candidate for that.' When they'd gone, she said to Marion Trimble, 'Is Jonah Kyte free?'

Marion consulted her terminal. 'Yes. He is.'

'Get him up here, will you?'

Jonah Kyte was a detective sergeant of imposing build and frightening good looks. When he arrived in the incident room, Susanna said, 'You were at the briefing?'

'Yes, ma'am.'

'Then you know that Terence Carpenter has been murdered. There were things we didn't know at the time of the briefing and we do know now. One is that Carpenter was gay. Another is that, some time before he died, he went to Number 26. Or, at least, he was delivered there by taxi. Number 26 need to be told. It may be too much to hope, but they may even have seen him leave and know someone was with him. Do you know the place?'

'I do, ma'am. And I'm sure lots of other officers know it, too.'

'Jonah, you're a valued member of Major Crimes and no one has the slightest interest in your life outside the police. And certainly not me. I'm not asking you to go to Number 26 because you're gay. I hope you know I wouldn't be so crass. What I'm asking is whether you know the management there?'

Somewhat mollified, Kyte nodded. 'I know the guy who runs it. If you think that would make it easier for me to gain his confidence, I'll go.'

'Thank you. I'd like you to tell them Carpenter is dead, tell them we are treating the death as suspicious, and see what they can tell us. All

44

right?'

'I'm on my way.'

As Jonah went out of the room, Susanna's phone rang. The caller said, 'Susanna. This is Bernie Spence. Short for Bernadette. I'm with the Post.'

'I know who you are. What I don't know is why you're calling me.'

'The same reason as I call most people. I'm following up a story. Looking for something that will interest our readers. The story in this case being the death of Terence Carpenter. What can you tell me?'

Susanna's tone was icy. 'Anything we have to say to the press will come from the press office. Who I'm quite sure have your contact details.'

'Look, Susanna, we can do it that way if you want. But that's a no favours approach.'

'And no favours are exactly what you can expect.'

'I didn't mean favours to me. I was talking about favours to you.' When Susanna said nothing, she went on, 'Look. You and your guys, you ask people questions. That's what you do. It's also what I do – I ask people questions, too. But there's a difference.'

'There certainly is. People who don't answer your questions are committing no offence. People who refuse to answer ours may be charged with obstructing the police in the course of their duty. That's a criminal offence. Police Act 1996,

Section 89, Subsection 2.'

'Yes, yes, Susanna, I know all about that. But you know the strange thing? Criminal offence or not, those same people are far more willing to answer questions asked by a journalist than those asked by the police. When the police ask something, the answer could get the person answering into trouble. Or get somebody else into trouble. But when I ask something, the person I'm talking to doesn't see magistrate's courts and police cells – they see fame. Their name in the papers. People talking about them. Being stopped in the street and asked their opinion by complete strangers, as though they were a celebrity. So the answers you get – if you get them at all – are likely to be evasive. Partial. Possibly even untrue.'

Susanna snorted. 'If I had a pound for every untrue answer I've ever been given…'

'Precisely. Whereas the answers I get… Well, they may exaggerate the importance of the person giving them, but they're usually pretty accurate. People don't want to see some lie they told reproduced in the press – their neighbours will know they lied and they'll think the less of them.'

Susanna said, 'Bernie, it's a good pitch. I'm impressed. But I can't talk to you. It really is the job of the press office. I can get into quite serious trouble if I tell you things.'

'Well. I did my best. You know, one of the most interesting sources for me is gossip. I'm going out there and I'm going to talk to people who knew

Terence Carpenter and some of what I hear will be gossip. And gossip can be extremely fruitful. It can lead me down alleys of enquiry that I would never otherwise have thought of. It could lead you down them, too. But, if you can't, you can't.'

Susanna said, 'I said I can't tell you things, Bernie. There's nothing to prevent you telling me things.'

'I should scratch your back even though you won't scratch mine? I'm sorry, Susanna – that's not the way the world turns. If it's any comfort, you'll be able to find out what people tell me. Just read the Post.'

CHAPTER 6

If Rayyan had been asked, he'd probably have said Carpenter's gardener was likely to be weather-beaten, filled with garden lore handed down by his father and grandfather, and bowed by age. In fact, Rupert Pateman was in his thirties and had interned for a year at Kew while taking a BSc in Plant Science at the University of Edinburgh. Rayyan said, 'That seems like a lot of education to end up looking after gardens in Parkside Avenue.'

'Thank you for the vote of confidence, Sergeant. In fact, you're right; my ambitions when I went to Edinburgh reached rather higher than this. But the National Trust and the big gardens are laying people off rather than taking them on and I'm afraid I didn't achieve the First I needed for a job in research. So it was either this or work for one of the multinationals doing their best to destroy the planet. On balance, I preferred this.'

Nicola said, 'How did you get on with Mr Carpenter?'

'As a garden owner, I found him ideal. He was always open to the idea of something new.'

'Especially if other people didn't have it?' asked Nicola.

Pateman came the closest he had to a smile since they'd arrived and introduced themselves. 'You obviously know gardeners. There is a great deal of one-upmanship, that's true. And Mr

Carpenter did like to have unusual plants that he could get written up in the journals. That was good for me, of course – I always got a mention.'

Rayyan said, 'So you liked him as a garden owner.'

'And I liked him rather less,' said Pateman, 'as a person.'

'Because…?'

'He wasn't mean. Far from it. He paid me well, and always on time. And if I suggested plant material or equipment, he never said no.'

'But…?'

Pateman seemed to be reflecting on how he should answer. After a long pause, he said, 'He made a pass at me. More than one. And I don't swing that way.'

Nicola said, 'Did he take no for an answer?'

'He did in the end, because I gave him no choice. Don't misunderstand me; if a man prefers other men as partners, I respect that. What I didn't like about Mr Carpenter's advances was that he seemed to feel he had a right to go on making them even when I'd made it clear I wasn't interested.'

'He was importunate,' said Rayyan.

'Nice word,' said Pateman. 'It fits.'

Nicola said, 'When did you last see him?'

'It must have been sometime last week.' He paused to think. 'Thursday. A week ago last Thursday. He came home from work early because he wanted to speak to me about installing new glass on the south facing wall. He fancied growing apricots there.'

'So you didn't see him all this week?'

'No. But that would be normal. He's a lawyer. He'd usually be working while I was here.'

Nicola said, 'What about when he paid you?'

'The money went straight from his bank account into mine. And the next payment isn't due for another two weeks.'

Rayyan said, 'Ms Carew is also your client. How do you get on with her?'

It would have been hard to miss the softening in the gardener's expression. He said, 'Very well. She is as unlike Carpenter as it's possible to be.'

'She doesn't share his garden snobbery?'

Pateman said, 'Snobbery? Is that what it is? Well, perhaps. From that point of view Ms Carew is a bust for any ambitious gardener. She likes all the traditional things her mother probably liked before her. A Gertrude Jekyll translated to the 21st century. You can imagine her training climbing roses around a Lutyens house.'

'Actually,' said Nicola, 'I can't. But then, I live in a second-floor maisonette.'

Rayyan said, 'So you like Ms Carew, but not only as a gardening client.'

'That's right. I also like Ms Carew as a person.'

Nicola said, 'Has she ever made a pass at you?'

'Or you at her?' said Rayyan.

'And in either case,' said Nicola, 'was the interest reciprocated?'

Pateman said, 'Those are improper questions.'

Rayyan said, 'Where were you last Friday and last Saturday?'

'Do you mean you don't actually know on what day Mr Carpenter died?'

'If you could answer the question,' said Rayyan.

'Very well. Fridays I work on Ms Carew's garden.'

'You weren't there today.'

'Yes, I was. I started at eight and finished at one. I don't know what time you got there, but it must have been after that.'

'And last Saturday?'

'I was at a shoot, about forty miles from here. I came home with two pheasants. Would you like the details?'

When Nicola had recorded everything he could tell her about the shoot, Rayyan thanked Pateman for his time. As they were about to leave, Pateman said, 'What happens now about Mr Carpenter's garden? Should I go on working there?'

'I've no idea, Mr Pateman. I suggest you speak to Mr Carpenter's partner. He is another Mr Carpenter.'

***

Nicola and Rayyan were already back at the station when Jonah Kyte returned from his visit to Number 26. 'The manager is sure Carpenter didn't come into the club last Friday. He'd have remembered him, because Carpenter would

51

usually spend a couple of hundred quid. And he was a good tipper. But last Friday he wasn't there. And I've been right through the CCTV film from before the taxi picked Carpenter up at home till an hour after he was dropped at the end of the street. He never came in. Whatever he did, he didn't reach Number 26.'

'Now there's a mystery,' said Susanna. 'Where did he go after the taxi dropped him off? Marion, we're going to need door-to-door in that street. And we also need to know if anyone around there has CCTV that might have picked him up.' She looked up as a uniformed constable entered the incident room. He said, 'Ma'am, there's a locksmith in reception. He says he was told to ask for you.'

Susanna said, 'Nicola, go down to reception and take this guy to Parkside Avenue. It's a crime scene, so you'll have to kit him out with protective gear. If he's able to open the safe, make sure he doesn't see what's in it. He wouldn't be the first locksmith to sell a story to the press that we'd rather keep secret.'

CHAPTER 7

He must have dozed off. He'd tried not to, but in vain. In fact, it felt as though he'd slipped into a coma. But it must be daytime because he could hear wings flapping above him. Birds – didn't they peck out the eyes of those who couldn't defend themselves? He shuddered. And then he heard sounds outside – boots scraping on stone and then a door opening. Light flooded in and he was temporarily too blinded to take in his surroundings in any detail. And then a man was kneeling beside him, and he sensed that this was the man who'd locked him in here. And what he realised then was that it was not a man. Maybe he'd been confused by light-headedness from lack of food, lack of water, discomfort and not enough sleep, but close-up there wasn't any doubt: this man was a woman. A mature woman, if he was being polite about it, and probably one who expected to get her way and usually did.

And then there was someone else in the room, and he knew who this was because it was the woman in the Renault, the girl from the recreation ground all those years ago. Rita. For a moment, the recollection of that shameful day overwhelmed him. He struggled to tell her how sorry he was, but when he tried to speak, his throat refused to cooperate and only meaningless sounds came out.

The woman was pouring liquid into a plastic

glass, which she held to Saville's lips. 'We've neglected you terribly. You must be feeling the thirst of the Connachts. Here. Let's get this down you.'

Saville had no idea what that reference to the Connachts was supposed to mean, but he had no time to think about it because he was drinking from the glass and he knew almost immediately that this was a mistake, but the woman had the glass tilted against his lips and was holding his nose closed so that he could only breathe through his mouth, and the liquid was pouring across his tongue and down his throat and into his stomach.

It was whisky. Scotch, not Irish – Saville had drunk enough of both to know the difference. And it was so, so warming that a sense of well-being flooded through him. Though that was probably not the whisky alone, because Saville had a good enough sense of taste in alcoholic matters to know that there was something else in the Scotch. Well-being had not been the right expression. Euphoric – that was how he felt.

The woman said, 'I expect you'd like something to eat. Well, let's leave that for now. There are other things to attend to.' She turned to Rita, who went out and came back carrying one of those big, black rubber things that gardeners use to carry waste in. A trug. The woman took out of it what looked like an outsize pair of secateurs or shears. Garden loppers. That's what they were. She removed Saville's shoes, and then his socks, and dropped them into the trug. Then she unzipped Saville's trousers and did the same with them. When it came to the boxer shorts, she said, 'Oh, dear. Had a bit of an accident, did you? Well, it will all be the same in a hundred years.' And the underpants, too, went into the trug.

It got more complicated from there, because undressing the upper half of Saville's body meant using the loppers – but Saville wasn't conscious of any of this because thanks to whatever had been in the whisky the euphoria had grown massively. He felt at ease and in love with the whole of the universe. This woman doing whatever it was she was doing was his friend. Rita was here and he knew that this feeling of euphoria could only mean that he was forgiven and he was so, so sorry for what they had done to her and so, so grateful that she held no grudges, and the world seemed a more wonderful place than it had been since he was a small child held and loved by his parents. Before they… Well. Before. There was no need to get into that stuff now.

When Saville was completely naked, Rita carried the trug and the shears outside. When the woman took secateurs and removed the cable ties that turned out to be what was securing Saville's wrists, something deep inside his muddled brain told him, if he was ever going to have a chance to escape, this was it. But Saville was incapable of moving. Nor did he feel any great urge to do so; if he'd been sufficiently conscious and capable of describing how he felt, he'd have said that he was swimming with dolphins – something he and Carol had once done on holiday in Florida – or flying with angels. When the woman gently laid him flat, instead of resisting he cooperated fully. She put something around his throat. What it was, Saville had no idea.

Now Rita moved in close beside him. Her hand gently touched his cheek. He said, 'Rita. I'm so, so sorry.'

'Are you, my sweet? Are you?' She pressed her face close to his. She kissed him gently. 'Don't worry about it now.' And then her hand was on his penis, and he could imagine nothing he wanted more, though how he would explain any of this to Carol when he got home was beyond him. But if Rita could forgive him, then surely Carol could do the same. If he'd felt able to move, he'd have restricted himself to snuggling up against Rita. There was a smile on his face.

And then, just as he felt his orgasm coming and no longer needed Rita's hand to help him reach the moment of nirvana, the other woman took hold of the two ends of whatever it was she'd put round Saville's throat and pulled, hard and unremittingly. And Saville's "petite mort" turned out to be not so little after all.

When he was still and it was clear that he would never move again, Rita smiled at her fellow murderer. 'Did you see the look on his face, right at the end? It seemed like he was saying, "What?

Who? Me? Now?"'

And she laughed.

* * *

DCI Bill Blazely came back from court in a very good mood having seen the judge sentence to ten years a villain Blazely had been pursuing on and off since he was a DC. 'When is the next briefing scheduled?'

'In the morning, sir,' said Susanna. '8 o'clock.'

'Okay, leave it that way. But give me my own mini-briefing right now. Tell me what you've got and what you're doing.' He listened to what Susanna had to say. 'Well, you seem to have everything under control. That's excellent. I promised the lads in the other team I'd help them celebrate today's victory, but you know how to get hold of me. Anything happens that needs my input, call me and I'll be right here. I mean it, Susanna – I know we haven't worked together, you and me, but day or night, you need me, just call.' And off he went to the pub where the ten-year sentence was being memorialised in beer.

Marion Trimble had watched this exchange without comment. When only she and Susanna were at their end of the room, she said, 'You should take that as a compliment.'

'I should?'

'If he didn't have complete faith in you, would he leave you on your own?'

'I'm almost persuaded, Marion. I'll suspend

final judgement until we've caught the murderer and we see who gets the credit.' She saw a DC walk in and set a coffee down beside his workstation. She called him over. To Marion she said, 'Have we got an action that someone can do from their desk?'

Marion looked at her screen. 'Terence Carpenter was born to a second wife. His brother suggested we should be looking at the first wife and her children. But you didn't see that they had any motive, ma'am.'

'I still don't,' said Susanna. She turned to the waiting detective. 'The wife is probably long dead. But it still needs to be crossed off the list, so see what you can do about tracking them down. Okay?'

Rayyan said, 'What have you got for me?'

'Go and grab a coffee. Relax for a few minutes till Nicola gets back. We'll all be begging for rest before we get away from here.'

* * *

And so they would, she thought. And what this time pressure did to relationships didn't bear thinking about. Everything she'd heard about high divorce rates among the police was anecdotal – it might be true, it might not, she had no way of knowing. But it was something extra a relationship had to bear.

Two weeks from now, she was due to go to a wedding as Chris McAvoy's significant other.

She'd be meeting the family of Chris's late wife. She didn't know how they would take to her, but she did know that she'd like to do everything possible to show she was treating the wedding – and them – with the proper respect. She'd planned to spend this weekend shopping for a new dress. Not much chance of that happening now. She'd also planned to have as much of the next two days as possible with him. They'd only been an item for four months and they were deep into that early relationship mixture of love and lust in which you occupy a bubble from which everyone else is excluded.

Being part of the Major Crime Investigation Team didn't make that possible. No one had any doubt about MCIT's priorities: catching a murderer took precedence over everything. She couldn't complain. This was what she'd wanted since she was a child. But sometimes it was hard.

She shook her head. Obsessing about something she couldn't change would get her nowhere.

* * *

The amount of equipment in the locksmith's van meant there was no point asking him to transfer to Nicola's car, so she said, 'I'll go with you to show you the way. You can drop me back here afterwards.' She brought with her into the van two sets of crime scene clothing.

As he drove she said, 'How did you get into the

59

locksmith business?'

'I'm not a locksmith. There's no point calling me if you lock yourself out of your house. My business card says I'm a licensed safe breaker. I worked for one of the big safe manufacturers for forty years. When it came time to retire, I decided I wasn't ready to do nothing, so I set up as a freelance. Most police forces in the country use me from time to time and all the safe manufacturers. Someone loses the key to their safe and they can't find a serial number so the maker can't send a replacement. Or they forget the combination. More often, the safe owner dies without telling anyone where to find the key or the combination. And sometimes it's a fire. If the fire is severe enough, the mechanism will be twisted and you can try all you like with a key or a combination; you just won't get in. Any of those things happen, they call for me.'

'And what do you do?'

'It depends on the problem. A lot of safes are opened with a key. In that case, the simplest thing is to find the key. First thing I do is turn the place over, looking for it. Same with the combination – the owner's dead, his heirs say he never wrote the combination down but it turns out he did. They just didn't look in the right places. Do a job like mine for long enough, you get to know where the right place is likely to be. You'd be amazed where some people hide a combination.'

'Our forensics people have turned this house

over. They're still doing it. They haven't been looking for a combination particularly; they look at everything. What do you do in a case like that?'

'If you look in the back of the van, you'll see an angle grinder and a lump hammer. Worst possible case means taking the angle grinder to the outside of the safe. Get through that, you'll often find a layer of concrete. I smash that up with a hammer. When the concrete is gone, you can see the inner safe and I use the angle grinder again on that. Cut a big enough hole, you can get your hand inside and scoop everything out. With any luck, it won't come to that today. The details I got say this is quite an old safe and not very expensive. That means it won't have lots of clever protection. You'd be amazed how often I can open a safe using a stethoscope to hear the tumblers as they fall. Let's hope for that, shall we?'

When they reached Parkside Avenue, Nicola led the way through the blue-and-white crime scene tape and handed him his protective gear. It was clear that this was far from the first time he'd put such things on. A PC was still on duty and he noted their arrival in the log. Only two SOCO workers were in the house. When she had shown the safe breaker where the safe was, he stood in the middle of the room, looking slowly around and taking everything in. It reminded Nicola of the DI when she first visited a crime scene. She'd seen Rayyan do the same thing and she was trying to develop the habit herself. At length, the safe breaker said he needed to turn the desk onto its side. Nicola said, 'We'd better get the SOCOs to do that.'

They came without argument and tipped the desk over as the safe breaker asked. He peered closely at the base of all four legs. Then he said, 'Have you got a notebook?'

Nicola took out the tablet that had replaced detectives' notebooks.

The safe breaker said, 'Left 3, Right 5. New group. Right 4, Right 2, Left 1.' After he'd read out two more groups, he said, 'I'd bet my pension on that being the combination. The only thing we don't know is the correct order for the four groups, so you'll have to try them one at a time. To save you the embarrassment of asking me to look away when you have the door open, I'm going to go outside and smoke a cigarette. If it takes you a long time, I'll smoke two. Come down for me when you're ready to go. I'll take you back to where I picked you up and you can sign my voucher so I get paid.'

Nicola stared at the SOCOs, who were lifting the table back into position. 'Anything to say, lads?'

'Yeah,' said one of them. 'We learned something new about where safe combinations can be hidden. Next time, we'll know.'

There was no point trying to score points off SOCO. They were immune to any kidding. The third trial combination of groups opened the safe.

Nicola photographed the interior before touching anything. Then she lifted out the contents one item at a time and began the process of logging each item, placing it inside an evidence bag and sealing the bag. There wasn't much, but what there was looked really interesting, and it couldn't be left here. Barney Carpenter seemed to be on the right wavelength, but when he was able to enter what was, after all, now going to be his house, would he do the right thing by the material his brother had kept in this safe? Or would he want to dispose of it to keep his brother's past secret?

That was not a chance Nicola intended to take. And she could, at least, by careful bagging and logging, make sure that no one could challenge the chain of evidence.

CHAPTER 8

There was no mistaking Nicola's excitement when she walked into the incident room. Susanna said, 'You've found something.' It wasn't a question.

'Yes I have. I don't know whether it has any bearing on Carpenter's death, but I do know it's a record of a serious offence.'

'Give the log to Marion. Let her enter it into HOLMES. I'll get Rayyan – I told him to take a break. Hold fire till he gets here.'

When Rayyan was back in the room, and Marion had got the whole of the exhibits log into HOLMES, Susanna said, 'Okay, Nicola. Let's see what has you so excited.'

Nicola picked up one of the evidence bags. They were all aware of a case that had failed in court only last year when the defence was able to challenge the chain of evidence for a vital exhibit because the evidence bag it was held in had been opened and closed several times in the same place and the various openings had not been logged. No-one here was going to make that mistake. When Nicola had bagged this item, she'd sealed the bag with a label on which she had written the date and time and her initials before sealing it. That same combination of date, time and initials was in the exhibits log. Now, she opened the bag by cutting it in a different place from where it had been sealed. Marion logged the time and date of

64

opening, the people present and the reason for opening the bag. Then Nicola extracted from the evidence bag the photograph she had sealed in it. She placed the photograph on the desk. Susanna said, 'I think I see what we are looking at, Nicola, but please describe it in your own words. Marion, make sure you log this.'

Nicola said, 'There are three men and a boy of about fifteen in this picture. The boy is face-down on a bed, but someone has raised his head so that he's looking at the camera. In my opinion, the man kneeling between his legs and apparently sodomising him is Terence Carpenter. I don't recognise any of the other men. The stamp on the back of the photograph says it was taken fifteen years ago.'

'Well done, Nicola,' said Susanna. 'Let's get some copies made of that photograph and then put it back in the evidence bag and re-seal it. While we are doing that, tell us what else you have – you don't need to open the bags just yet.'

Nicola said, 'There's a separate photograph from what looks like an amateur dramatics group's programme. I don't think there's any doubt that the boy in the photograph is the boy being sodomised by Carpenter. The programme gives his name as Rigby Hewitt. And there are some other photographs of men in apparently homosexual activities.'

Susanna said, 'Marion, some new actions, please. The first thing we need to do is find out who Rigby Hewitt is and where he is now. The second is to get those photographs to a fingerprint technician. We have Carpenter's fingerprints from the post-mortem. I want confirmation that his prints are on the photographs, but I also want to know whether there are any other prints there and whether whoever they belong to is known to us. One other thing. Did we assign anyone to look into Cyril Bonser's background and private life?'

Marion Trimble shook her head. 'I'll create an action.'

'Please do. Nicola, put one of the copies of the first photograph on the whiteboard. We are going to have to open all the photographs, copy them all, and put the copies on the board. Please take great care – we don't want a defence lawyer getting the killer off because we messed up the chain of evidence.' She looked at her watch. 'Where the hell does the time go? Look, we're all tired and most of these actions can't be done when offices are closed. Let's take a break. Have something to eat and get some sleep. I want everyone back here at eight tomorrow morning, refreshed and ready to go. Nicola and Marian, before you go, take all those evidence bags to the Major Incidents Exhibit Store and get them signed for.'

They were about to go their separate ways when the door opened and DCI Blazeley came in. Nicola said, 'Good evening, Sir. Celebrations over?'

'I imagine some people are still whooping it up, but I had a phone call. They rang me because I'm

SIO on the Carpenter case – so it affects you.'
Every head was now turned to face Blazeley, and
no one was any longer moving towards the door.
He said, 'The call was from West Mercia.
Shropshire have got a body found in similar
circumstances to ours, right down to the semen left
on it. The DI's name there is Golding. His first
name is Charles, but everyone calls him William.
They must be literary types in Shropshire. I've
agreed the cases are linked so we are taking
primacy for their investigation too. Give him a
call, Susanna. I'd like it to be you who makes the
first visit – take someone with you if you like, but
don't delegate. This is too important for that.
Golding is based at Shrewsbury, but he says drive
to Oswestry and he'll meet you at the police
station there. Oh – and he says you'll need wellies.
And apparently the death is right out in the sticks.
The only light at this time of day would be from
the moon. He's expecting you in the morning.'

Susanna looked around at the team. 'Okay. I
said I wanted everyone here at eight tomorrow
morning. Change that to six thirty. Now go, have
something to eat and get your heads down.
Tomorrow is likely to be a long day.'

'Yes, it is,' said Blazeley. 'But there's no need
to make it worse for you. You go to Oswestry and
see Golding. I'll take the briefing tomorrow
morning.' He looked around. 'And I'll give you all
a break. Instead of six thirty, get here by seven.
And make sure everyone who needs to be here gets

that message. I'll arrange bacon sandwiches and coffee.'

Susanna said, 'Thank you, sir. I'll go to Oswestry on my own. That way, everyone with something to contribute to tomorrow's briefing will be here.'

***

When Nicola had followed Susanna's instructions about the exhibits, she left the station with Rayyan just ahead of her. The day had been so frenzied that she had completely forgotten that tomorrow she was supposed to attend what her married sister, Sasha, had called a "dinner party." She knew without having asked that there'd be a single man there. A man that Sasha thought would be a perfect fit for her. A man that Nicola would really prefer not to meet. And now she need not! With a lightening heart, she texted her sister to say she was involved in a murder investigation, that she was just finishing work today having started early that morning, that the same would be true tomorrow, and that she had to bow out of all personal commitments until the case was solved.

A murder investigation. Now there was a thought. She'd been on the fringes of a few while she'd been in uniform, of course. Going door-to-door. Keeping crime scenes clear of people not authorised to be there. She'd been a detective for a while now, but she was new to the major crime team. She didn't think she would ever become blasé about murder, however long she stayed with the team, but right now she was excited in a way that meant she really did not want to spend the evening chatting to her lodger while the TV prattled in the background. She made the effort to catch up with Rayyan. 'Any plans for the evening?'

Rayyan shook his head. 'There isn't much evening left. I don't think I can be bothered to cook. And I don't feel like sitting in a restaurant surrounded by other people. I might pick up a pizza on the way home. You?'

'Much the same. And yet, my head is buzzing too much to be able to slob out in front of the box with a lodger yakking at me. Bear in mind, I'm new to major crime. Pizza sounds like a good idea. Maybe we could get two, and some Peronis. Eat them together?'

'I could go for that. Your place or mine?'

'Sarge. I have a flatmate. She's there because without her I couldn't pay the mortgage. And you, I think, live on your own.'

'My place it is,' said Rayyan. 'Why don't you follow me? There's a good place for pizza on the way.'

* * *

When they reached Rayyan's house, Nicola discovered they could both park in his driveway. Had they gone to her maisonette, finding parking spaces for two cars would have been a problem.

Even parking one car was often not easy. In the kitchen, she said, 'How do you afford a place this size?'

'My parents are both dead. They had a perfectly ordinary four-bedroom house, but they'd owned it for thirty years and it was in Richmond. House prices in that part of Surrey are ludicrous compared with here. They left everything equally to me and my brother. He lives in Ealing now so even with his share he still needed a mortgage, but me, I moved out here and found myself with enough to buy this place for cash. I haven't furnished every room yet; I'm working on that. Open two beers, will you?' He pointed to a cupboard. 'If you want to drink yours out of a glass, you'll find them in there. Stick the other four beers in the fridge. I'll just slice up these pizzas and put them on plates. I hope you don't mind pieces of kitchen roll instead of napkins?'

They chatted about the case over pizza and beer. When Rayyan grinned it was, Nicola thought, a completely transforming grin that turned a work colleague into the boy next door. There were so many things about him she wanted to know but couldn't ask. Things like: What was it like growing up in this country when you looked so different from the people around you? She knew he was the son of an English academic who had taught for a few years at a university in Malaysia and married a woman from there. But how did something like that affect your childhood? Maybe one day their relationship would be such that she could ask. But that wasn't the case right now.

When the pizzas had been eaten and the beers had been drunk, there was nothing to keep Nicola there any longer. Not unless she manufactured it. She'd always liked Rayyan in the sense of someone it was good to work with. Someone with a sense of humour. Someone who saw a lot of things much as she did. Someone who didn't allow insecurities about his position to prevent him being a warm and supportive colleague. Did she, perhaps, like him rather more than that, and in a completely different way? And, if she did, what where his views on the subject?

She was tempted to ask whether his failure yet to furnish all of the rooms meant that there was only one bed. And, if so, how big it was.

And then common sense re-established itself. She said, 'Thanks for the company, Rayyan. I really wouldn't have wanted to spend a vacuous evening with Cheryl after what we've been through today.' She stood up, and Rayyan stood with her. Was that just a trace of disappointment on his face? Or was she imagining it, seeing something that she wanted to be there, even though it wasn't? It was hard enough reading the face of a fellow English person, without trying to find a way through that oriental inscrutability. And as soon as she'd had the thought, she mentally slapped herself – Rayyan was as English as she was. She stepped forward and kissed him lightly on the cheek. 'I'd better take it easy on the way home. I don't want to be breathalysed after three beers. I'll see you tomorrow at the briefing.'

***

Susanna picked up fish and chips and then drove home to the three-bedroom house she occupied on her own where she ate the fish supper, showered, changed, and slipped a clean pair of knickers into her bag. She wasn't planning to come back here till morning. Then she drove to Superintendent McAvoy's somewhat larger house.

'Susanna! You made it! Have you eaten?'

'I have.' She snuggled into his arm in a way that would once have been anathema but that now she found natural. 'Would you think me awful if I wanted to be horizontal for a while?'

It was not until sometime later that they came downstairs again, Susanna in nothing but one of McAvoy's T-shirts which stretched halfway down her thighs and the superintendent in a pair of boxer shorts. He poured them both a glass of red wine. Susanna sniffed hers and then took a large sip which she held for a moment in her mouth before swallowing. She said, 'This is good.'

'I planned to serve it with the cassoulet. But I have another bottle. In fact, I have five. There was an offer on a half-dozen that I felt unable to refuse.'

She snuggled closer. And then she raised the

question that had brought her here. If she hadn't wanted to talk about this, she'd have told Chris that tomorrow's early start meant she needed to stay home and go to bed. She said, 'Can we discuss this wedding I'm going to? Specifically, the question of a present?'

'I've already bought it, Suze. I sent it from both of us. But that isn't really what's bothering you, is it?'

'No.' How was she going to approach this? In the end, she decided to use her normal direct bull-at-a-gate method. 'Chris. If Paula hadn't died, you wouldn't be going with me. You'd be going with her.'

'Yes. And?'

'You were married to her for fifteen years. Fifteen happy years.'

'Yes, I was. No marriage is perfect, but ours was better than most. Apart from the fact that she couldn't have children – but that wasn't her fault. And now it was probably for the best.'

'And then she died. Of an aneurism that came right out of the blue. A complete shock. And you grieved for her for five years.'

'Yes. I did. And I won't pretend otherwise: I grieve for her still. But you know what? Life continues. When something like that happens, you think it's all over. You'll never be happy again. I can just imagine what I was like to work for when I came back from compassionate leave.'

'Which most people would say you did too

soon.'

'Most people who haven't suffered that kind of loss. Looking back to that time, I don't think there's much doubt that I was a crazy man. And you get over it. If people think that's callous, let them. There's a life spirit in each one of us that drives us onwards. And then I met you.'

'And that's what concerns me. Two weeks from now we are going to the wedding of the eldest son of Paula's older sister.'

'Maria. That's right.'

'At least, we are if we've broken the back of Terence Carpenter's murder. How is Maria going to react to me?'

'Well. Why don't you turn that question around? Imagine that you are Maria. That it was your sister who died. That her husband, your brother-in-law, grieved for your sister for five solid years. And then he found someone he could be happy with again. And you are about to meet that someone. How would you react to her?'

Susanna stared at him in silence. Then, smiling, she held out her glass. 'May I have another?'

When Chris raised the bottle she said, 'But make it a small one. I have to be on the road to Shropshire early tomorrow. And before that, I have to get home and change.'

CHAPTER 9

There was something almost shy about Rita's expression as she showed Deborah the drawing. Why she felt this uncertainty about her talent, Deborah had no idea. 'It's brilliant,' she said.

'Do you really think so?'

'You've caught him exactly. I can almost see the soul leaving his body. And the look on his face. How did you describe it? As if he was saying, "Who? What? Me? Now?" That's exactly how you've made him look. I love it.'

'I don't think that's a soul you can almost see, Deborah. I don't think he had one of those. If he did, I can tell you where it is right now. It's somewhere very hot. I'll put this one with the one of Carpenter.' She knelt by Deborah's chair. 'Two down. One to go. Carpenter and Saville...' She wiped a hand across her throat in the traditional "end it" gesture. 'That leaves Ralph Townsend. When do you think we'll do him?'

Deborah cupped Rita's cheek in her hand and kissed her. 'As soon as I find out where he is, we'll start making plans. We don't want to rush it. Do we?'

Rita wrapped her arms around Deborah. 'Oh, no, we don't. It's taking time to think about what we're going to do that makes it as lovely as it is. I don't want to give up any of that.'

'That's right, my cherub. Anticipation. In many

ways, anticipation is better than the act itself.'

'Oh, I don't think so, Deborah. It's very good. It's part of the pleasure of removing one of those horrible men from the surface of the earth. But it isn't the best bit.'

Deborah laughed. 'What is the best bit, my angel?'

'Watching them go. Right at the end, when they are so loving what I'm doing to them, loving it so much they must feel like they're in heaven, and then you send them to hell. That's the best bit. There could never be anything else quite that good. But thinking about it before we do it… Yes, that's almost up there with the best.'

* * *

Susanna rolled out of bed at four the next morning, moving as quietly as she could in order not to wake Chris. She dressed, went stealthily downstairs and let herself out. There was just time now to get home, shower, change her clothes, breakfast on toast and marmalade with a mug of tea, and set off for Shropshire. In the car on her way home she pondered last night's conversation about the wedding. There was one thing she hadn't mentioned and it was going to trouble her. She still didn't have a dress to match the occasion and if they didn't get a breakthrough soon in the Carpenter murder she didn't see how she would ever have time to look for one. And how would she find time to have her hair done?

Common sense said that these were peripheral matters and unimportant in the great scheme of things. But common sense doesn't get a look in when you're about to meet your lover's family for the first time.

***

Bill Blazeley had kept his promise about the bacon sandwiches. When everyone turned up at seven, Bill had already been there for half an hour, reading the HOLMES log so that he was up to date and ready to lead a briefing. He said, 'Okay; you all know what you're doing, so let's get on with it. A word before we start. We have HOLMES, and HOLMES is a huge advantage in the fight against crime but it won't do our job for us. What it does is make sure nothing is missed. We are still the detectives and we still have to remember the first three questions that should come to us as second nature every time we visit the scene of a murder. Why this person? Why here? Why now? Find the answers to those questions and you'll find the killer. And the three questions come with three rules attached – the detective's ABC. Assume nothing. Believe nobody. Check everything.' He looked at the HOLMES log he had printed out. 'Gareth, according to this print out, you were allocated the task of tracking down Terence Carpenter's first family.'

'Yes, sir. That was pretty straightforward; the General Register Office keeps information online and anyone can look it up. So…' He took out his tablet. 'According to the registration of Terence's birth, his father was Walter Carpenter. That record also gives the name of his mother, but what I was looking for was the wife before her. Walter Carpenter fathered two boys and a girl by his first wife – I'll give you this when I'm finished, Marion, so you can get it all logged on HOLMES. The first wife's surname was Muir – the birth index only gives the mother's surname and not her first name. She's been dead for thirty years, so whoever we're looking for it isn't her. The daughter's name was Credenza. Credenza Carpenter.' He stopped speaking and looked around.

Blazeley said, 'Credenza? They named her after a piece of furniture?'

'That's what the index says, sir.'

'Bloody hell,' muttered a constable.

'I suppose,' said Rayyan, 'they might not have known what it meant, and just liked the word.'

Nicola said, 'Or Walter might have just made a killing on a credenza and wanted to immortalise it.'

'We can't know the reason at this distance,' said Blazeley. 'Carry on, Gareth.'

'Yes, sir. I added sixteen years to the year she was born and I searched for the marriage of a Credenza Carpenter from that date forward. Nothing. There's no record of the marriage of a Credenza Carpenter at any time.'

Blazeley said, 'That isn't necessarily the end of the matter, of course. She might have emigrated and married elsewhere, or she might be dead. Or she might just have changed her name – you could hardly blame her.'

'I did search the deaths index, sir,' said Gareth. 'If she had emigrated and then died in another country, the death would not be recorded here. But there's no death in the UK of a Credenza Carpenter. I haven't yet had time to do a Google search for her or her two brothers, and nor have I searched Facebook or LinkedIn. Those are clearly the next tasks, but I'm on interview duty this morning on a different case so I'll have to leave them to someone else. In fact, sir, I really need to be starting the preparation for that interview, so…?'

'Yes,' said Blazeley, 'you be off. Thanks for all your help, but your main job is interviews. And nobody does it better,' he added. 'Marion, allocate those tasks to Nicola. Right. Who's next?'

***

Golding, a balding man in his forties, looked more like a farmer than a detective. It became clear as the visit went on that underestimating him would be a mistake. He said, 'We have to go out of town. If it was any further West, you'd be talking to the Heddlu and not to me.'

'Heddlu?' said Susanna.

'The Welsh police. Don't worry – they speak

79

English. After a fashion, anyway. I've borrowed a Land Rover from the locals. I suggest you leave your car in the car park behind the station.'

They headed west and then south. Golding said, 'We're following the Montgomery Canal. You'll be told that it's known locally as the Monty but I've never heard a single person from round here call it that. Head a few miles east and it joins the Ellesmere Canal and becomes part of the Shropshire Union system. A lot of the canal there has been restored for tourism and the restoration is gradually working its way south-west. Eventually, it will reach Newtown, just as the canal did in its heyday when it was used for transporting heavy goods.' The road branched and became narrower and then branched and became narrower again. At last, Golding turned through a gate into a farmer's fields. Golding said, 'See that humpbacked bridge? That goes over the canal. We'll park there.'

He tucked the Land Rover neatly into the lee of the hedge that they could now see ran along the northern side of the canal. Golding said, 'We've got to walk a little way, but the towpath is on the other side of the bridge. We need to suit up. Come round the back of the Land Rover – I've got protective gear in there. We can carry the overshoes – you need your wellies on until we reach the site.' When they were suited and booted, he led her over the bridge and turned right.

Susanna said, 'Where are we?'

'You're in God's own country. But don't tell people; the locals aren't particularly friendly towards tourists. But to answer your question, the nearest place of any size is Llynclys. And if you think that sounds Welsh, I understand, but it's actually in England. The Marches were fought over for hundreds of years after the Angles and the Saxons drove the natives back into Wales and Cornwall and the Scottish highlands. And the Vikings, of course, they spilled a bit of blood around here, just like they did everywhere else. And then the Normans arrived. Loved a fight, the Normans did. The border moved back and forth between England and Wales, so you've got places that you can tell by the name can only be Welsh but in fact they're in England – and that goes the other way round, too. Watch your feet here. Further back towards Maesbury Marsh the canal and the towpath have both been renovated and you can walk, cycle or canoe to your heart's content. This stretch is next to be done, and that's how the body was found. A crew of volunteers turned up this morning. They were supposed to store their gear in the old canal worker's cottage I'm taking you to. When they opened it up, they got a bit of a shock and they called us.'

Susanna said, 'I don't suppose the body is still there?'

'I'm afraid not. I confirmed that life was extinct, we photographed the body in situ and had it taken away. When I got back to the station and said what I'd found, one of our constables told me about your case.'

'I wonder how he knew?'

Golding shrugged. 'He's been around a long time. Knows a lot of people. I'm sure I don't have to tell you how news travels in our business. So, I'm sorry, but you can't see the body where we found it. The pathologist was going to start on the post-mortem straight away, but when I realised another force was involved I asked him to wait. It will only take us an hour to get to the Royal Shrewsbury Hospital and if we go when we are done here, he'll drop what he's doing and start the PM.'

'That would be great – get it all done today. Have we identified the body?'

'Not to this point. We've taken a photograph of the face and released it to the press office. It will be in the Shropshire Star this evening and the Border Counties Advertiser on Wednesday. It's already on both papers' websites and ours. If he's local, someone knows him.'

They'd been walking all through this and now they had reached a rather battered building. Golding said, 'This is the place. Amazing as it may seem, a canal worker once lived here with his wife and five children. God knows where they all slept. But that was a very long time ago. For at least the last sixty years, the farmer who farms these acres has used it for storage. Come back in two or three years, it will be a holiday rental. Or so they told me this morning.'

Susanna had to balance against the wall to change her Wellington boots for forensics booties. She opened the door and peered inside. This could be made into a place that people would pay to stay in for their holidays? Well... Maybe. She wasn't sure she could visualise it herself.

The woman in protective clothing who looked up from the doorway into what must once have been a kitchen smiled a welcome. 'We've found very little.' She pointed at a vertical metal pole that stretched from floor to ceiling. 'That, I think, is not an original part of the structure; it was put in to prevent the ceiling from collapsing. Someone has been bound to it – by what, we don't know. And for quite some time because the signs of where they've struggled to get free are evident. We've taken photographs. We've looked for fingerprints and found a huge number but who knows whether any of them are recent? Something has been spilled and then cleaned up; we think it was whisky. We've taken samples to check. Other than that – nothing.'

Susanna walked all the way around the ground floor. The state of the stairs made it clear that venturing to the second floor would be very risky. The forensic officer saw her looking and said, 'If you want my opinion, those stairs and the second floor have not been used by any human for a very long time.'

'Anything non-human?'

'There are droppings from a range of animals. We're pretty sure they include fox, rabbit, stoat, and badger. The badger just down here, obviously. We've taken samples to make sure. And birds have nested up there.'

Susanna turned to DI Golding. 'Has anyone talked to the farmer?'

'I did, this morning. Briefly. He rents these two fields to someone best described as a hippy. The hippy is known to us. He planned to hold music festivals there but it didn't work out. He's talking about installing glampods, but that won't work out, either. He's sublet a few times as camping spaces. Scouts, that sort of thing. I've got a DC going through his records right now. He finds anything, I'll let you know. But the first impression he gave me is that hippy bookkeeping is not the best. Now, if you've seen everything you want to see, we'll head for Shrewsbury. As soon as I have a signal, I'll tell the pathologist we're on our way.'

CHAPTER 10

The last action agreed at the morning briefing went to Rayyan. It was to answer the question: Where was Rigby Hewitt now? He and Nicola sat side by side at adjacent workstations; both began by pulling up the Google search page. They worked in silence for half an hour. Then Nicola said, 'I'm going for coffee. Want one?'

'I'd love one, thanks.'

When she brought the coffees back, Nicola said, 'Have you found anything?'

'Possibly. There's a Canadian actor called Rigby Hewitt. Is he our Rigby Hewitt? I thought our Rigby Hewitt might quite possibly be dead. Raped and then murdered. How many times in training are we told to assume nothing? And yet, we do. I was jumping ahead and thinking Terence Carpenter was murdered in revenge for Rigby's death. The only birth I can find of a Rigby Hewitt was in 1985 and it was here in Batterton. Is he also the Canadian Rigby Hewitt? We need to know.'

'What do we know about the local one?'

'He was illegitimate. Who his father might have been, I have no idea, but his mother was Cadie Hewitt, twenty-five, a graduate who'd just joined Reckitt and Colman as a research chemist – so this was no young girl taken advantage of and then deserted. If he was born in 1985, he's in his 30s now, and so is the Canadian. I used the same

General Register Office online records that Gareth used and there is no marriage for a Rigby Hewitt, and no death. I've asked DVLC whether there's a driving licence in that name, and I've also asked whether he has a passport. Those are both questions to public sector bodies, so we know how long it's likely to take to get an answer. The Canadian Rigby Hewitt is listed on the website of a Canadian acting agency. There's no photograph, which is odd for an actor's agent.'

'Maybe he isn't well known. Doesn't get much work.'

'Maybe. I've emailed the agency and said I want to speak to someone. They're in Toronto, so five hours behind us. With any luck I'll hear from them soon. I'm going to ask if the actor was born in Britain, and can I have a photograph? That's where I'm up to. How about you? What have you turned up?'

'I haven't found Credenza,' said Nicola, 'but one of the brothers is on Facebook and the other is on LinkedIn. I've messaged both of them to say I'd like to speak to them. I haven't said what it's about.' She took a sip from her coffee and looked at her terminal. 'And one of them replied as I spoke those words. I asked if I could have a phone number and he's given me one. Excuse me, Sarge.' She picked up her phone and dialled. A short pause and then, 'Is that Gary Carpenter? Hi, Gary. I'm the detective who contacted you on Facebook. Thank you for getting back to me.

86

Gary, I have some bad news for you. Terence Carpenter is dead. Terence. Your half-brother, Gary. Yes, I see. Gary, I understand that, but it isn't quite that simple. The death is suspicious. Yes, I'm saying that someone killed your half-brother.' There was a long pause as she listened to Gary Carpenter's lengthy response, during which she jotted down phrases. Then she said, 'Gary, I understand your position but when a suspicious death occurs all avenues have to be followed. We would not be doing our job otherwise. Now, could you please tell me how to contact your brother and your sister? Yes, Gary I have no doubt that you will let your brother know yourself, but I need to be in touch with them, too. So, where… Oh. I see. No contact at all? Well, it's a shame when families break up like that. But your brother?' She scribbled rapidly and then said, 'Thank you, Gary. That's very helpful. And can I please have your address? Gary… Thank you.' Once again, she was scribbling furiously. Then she said, 'I'm going to call your brother now. If you think of any way that I might be able to get in touch with Credenza, starting with what she calls herself now because it doesn't seem to be by that name, I'd be very grateful if you would get back to me.' She put down the phone and blew out her cheeks.

'Not very helpful?' asked Rayyan.

'He had no contact with his father after his father divorced his mother. He wasn't aware that he had any half siblings. I don't believe that for a moment, by the way. But, now that he does know and I've told him that one of them has been murdered, his reaction is,' she picked up the notes she had been writing, 'and I quote: "I really don't give two shakes of a gnat's cock." As for the sister, he and his brother lost touch with her years ago and it seems he does care about that.'

***

It was a long time since Susanna had gagged at a post-mortem, and she wasn't going to start now. She hadn't met this pathologist before, but every pathologist she had seen had impressed her with their professionalism and this one was no different. When he was cutting into the dead man's stomach, he said, 'Whisky. You probably can't smell it in the viewing area, but close up the smell is almost overwhelming. He must have been drinking on an empty stomach. There's no sign that he'd eaten anything for a long time. Judging by the marks on his wrists, he's been held prisoner for a while, with nothing to eat and, judging by the state of him, nothing to drink. If you want my off the record opinion, I'd say that if he'd been left another day he'd have died of thirst.' He looked up. 'That won't be in my written report.'

Susanna had expected nothing else. She'd always found pathologists to be helpful and they would make verbal observations the way this one just had to assist detectives who had a case to solve. What they would not do was put in writing anything they could not back up with hard evidence if called on. Susanna understood that – like murder detectives, pathologists didn't get involved in many cases before they had to stand up in court and justify the evidence they had given under cross-examination by a highly skilled defence barrister whose only concern was to get the defendant off, guilty or not. When the pathologist said, "That won't be in my written report," what he was really saying was, 'I'm telling you this because it may help your investigation but don't rely on it, because if we ever get into court I will have no recollection whatsoever of having said it and, if you quote me, I'll deny it.' They both knew that wouldn't happen, because the unbreakable rule of every barrister in the land was: If you don't know what the answer is going to be, don't ask the question.

***

At much the same time as Susanna was watching the pathologist cut up a dead man whose name she did not as yet know, Nicola was taking a call from her sister about the dinner date that she was going to miss that evening. She said, 'You do understand, Sasha, don't you?'

'I understand completely,' said her sister. 'You have absolutely no choice. But it isn't my understanding you need, is it? Our mother is going to think you've done this to spite her.'

Nicola laughed. 'I'm not responsible for

Mummy's dreams about my future. And neither are you. If she'd had anything to do with it, I'd never have gone anywhere near the police. The only thing that would really satisfy her is for me to leave the force, marry some well-paid guy and raise her grandchildren. You've already done that – I mean the well-paid guy and the grandchildren, not the police – but that doesn't satisfy her. Face it, she doesn't like telling her friends that one of her daughters does such a sordid job.'

Sasha said, 'Leave Mummy to me. But you would have liked this guy. He looks like George Clooney did when George Clooney looked like George Clooney.'

'Hey, Sis – as far as I'm concerned, George Clooney still looks exactly like himself. Any time you can line him up as my dinner party partner, just let me know and I'll pull a sicky here. As long as there isn't a murder enquiry on.'

Now it was Sasha's turn to laugh. 'I just wanted you to know that I understand, I'm not cross, and I'll handle our mother. Oh – and to let you know you are missing a truly fabulous dinner. I'm having it catered.'

'You're not!'

'I am. There's a firm does a lot of work for Kevin's bank. He let them know the bank was going out to tender and it wouldn't do their chances any harm if they took care of this evening for us.'

'Sasha, that's corruption!'

'So book me. It's the way of the world, sweetie. I'll put some of this fabulous meal in a doggy bag for you and keep it in the fridge. But collect it before tomorrow evening or I won't be able to resist it.'

When Nicola had finished this conversation, she found Rayyan looking at her, his expression unreadable. 'A George Clooney lookalike, eh?'

'My sister is given to hyperbole.'

'I'm sorry you're missing a dinner party.'

'I'm not. As I said, this is my first murder as a detective. I know it's terrible, because someone had to die to make it possible, but it's why we want to be in MCIT, isn't it? Anyway, I had my dinner party last night.'

'Pizza and Peroni?'

'Ah,' said Nicola, 'but I couldn't have had better company.' She winked at him, confident that he would take her words as a joke. And so they were – to a point. Where that point was, Nicola chose not to ask herself.

***

Rayyan's interest in Nicola's private life was interrupted by the arrival of an email. He said, 'It's the agent in Canada. He wants me to call him.' Nicola moved a little away from her own workstation, intent on what she might pick up from Rayyan's conversation.

The agent was very cagey. 'Tell me why you're enquiring about my client, Sergeant.'

'His name has come up in relation to an enquiry here.'

'His name.'

'His name. And that's all what we have, right now. We don't even know whether it's the same Rigby Hewitt. Can you tell me, was your client born in Canada, or here?'

'He was born in the UK, Sergeant. Does that help you?'

'It does. Thank you. Do you have a photograph you could send me?'

'Probably. Would you mind telling me what your case involves?'

'It's a murder.'

'A murder? In the UK? And you think Rigby might have been involved?'

'It's become clear that someone called Rigby Hewitt was known to the dead man at some time in the past. I'm afraid that's what most police work is like – we follow up every lead until it turns into a dead end, and the one that doesn't become a dead end tends to be the one we want. It can take a long time. A photograph?'

He could hear the sounds of something going on at the other end of the phone. Then the agent said, 'I've emailed one. It should arrive at any moment.'

'Do you have contact details for Rigby? I'd like to speak to him.'

'I do, and I'll email them to you, but I'm afraid you won't be able to speak for a few days. He's on location in the Yukon. I think he'll be back at the end of next week, but while he's up there there's no cell phone connection.'

'There is some urgency about this… Surely, wherever he is, there must be some way of contacting them?'

'I'm sure the lodge where they are staying has a satellite phone. The problem with those is that there is no privacy. Anyone in the vicinity will be able to hear what Rigby is telling you.'

'Nevertheless…'

There was a sigh, and then the agent said, 'I'll tell you what I'll do. I'll let Rigby know that you want to speak to him, and why. I'll give him your phone number and email. If he is willing to speak before he gets back to Toronto, he'll contact you.'

After the agent had hung up, Rayyan checked his emails and found the photograph of Rigby Hewitt. He put it up on his screen. 'He's an adult now. But just think for a moment what that face might have been like as a teenager. Then think about the picture of the youth Carpenter was buggering.'

'It could be him,' said Nicola.

'Couldn't it? We need to speak to Rigby Hewitt, as soon as possible, privacy or no privacy.'

CHAPTER 11

The post-mortem over, Susanna was about to leave when Inspector Golding's phone buzzed. After he'd taken the call, he said, 'You'd better come to the station with me.'

'Something's happened?'

'We know now who the dead man is. Ben Manfredi has come down from Oswestry. He's waiting for us.' Susanna's face expressed interest, and Golding said, 'Don't let the name fool you. Ben is short for Benito. His grandfather was a prisoner of war who stayed on when the war was over. You might think all the Italian POWs started ice cream parlours, but Ben's grandfather married a local farmer's daughter and inherited the farm. Ben's father took it over, but Ben has an older brother, so the brother became the farmer and Ben joined the police. He's with us for another three months. If he didn't have to, he wouldn't be retiring even then. But he knows everyone for miles around. He is the one who told me about your case. He recognised the body in the photo. But here we are at the station, so I'll let him tell you.'

Ben Manfredi looked as though he should have become the farmer. His angular, sunburned face belonged on someone growing olives in Tuscany, but his accent when he spoke was pure North Shropshire. He said, 'Michael Saville. That's your corpse. A good man. He'll be missed.'

'Say some more,' said Susanna.

'Not local. Came here after university as a teacher. Taught for, what? Twenty years, give or take. Taught my children, as it happens. They thought the world of him, and as far as I know so did everybody else.'

'Not everybody, it seems,' said Susanna.

'No,' Manfredi agreed. 'But I think there'll be general surprise when this gets out. You know how everyone says, "He always seemed like such a good person"? This time, they'll mean it.'

'Was he married?'

'I don't think they ever married, but he and Carol Watts have lived together for years. No children. I'd like to be the one who tells Carol, Boss. And I don't think we should leave it. You know how news spreads around here. I don't want her to hear it from someone else.'

Susanna said, 'Okay if I go with you?'

Manfredi looked towards Golding, who nodded. 'I don't see that that's a problem. What I'm more concerned about is that I go through the logs each morning and I don't remember seeing Saville reported missing. Find out why, Ben.'

Susanna said, 'You said he taught for about twenty years. He'd retired?'

'Packed it in. An awful lot of teachers these days seem to find they've had enough. He went to work for an adventure company. Camping for kids, Duke of Edinburgh's award, the Three

Peaks, Snowdon the hard way – you know the sort of thing. Carol's a dentist's receptionist. She'll be at home today – shall we go see her now?'

***

Deborah took a mobile phone from the table. 'I thought you'd like to hear this. It's Saville's phone. It was in his car when we took him out of it.'

Rita said, 'You want to get rid of that. 'If the cops find it on you…'

'The cops aren't anywhere near talking to me. Or you. Listen, will you?' She pressed a button.

'Saville? Are you there? It's Howard. Howard Diller. If you're there, pick up.'

Silence followed.

'Saville? We need to speak. Did you hear about Carpenter? Listen, I know it could be chance. Probably is. But it just might… We need to talk, Saville. Work out a plan. Just in case. Maybe talk to the police.'

More silence.

'Call me, Saville. For fuck's sake, call me.'

'So,' said Deborah. 'That isn't by any means the only message on there. There are five from somebody called Carol, wanting with increasing fury to know where the hell he thinks he is. But that one – what do you make of that one?'

'Who is Howard Diller?'

'He's the man who called Saville. Apart from that, I haven't a clue who he is – but I do know he

96

and Saville and Carpenter were in something together and he's frightened.'

'But what is he to us? He wasn't one of the ones… Why are you smiling, Deborah? I hate it when you smile like that. It's as though you know something I don't know.'

'You said it. He wasn't one of the ones. He didn't attack my darling love and he isn't on our list for vengeance. So if we add him to the list…'

'But why would we?'

'Rita. Carpenter is dead. Saville is dead. The police will take one look at the two bodies and know whoever killed Carpenter killed Saville. So what are they going to be looking for?'

Rita nodded. It irritated her when Deborah's thinking seemed brighter than hers – more intuitive, more inventive, more creative – but she knew it was also one of the things that had brought them together in the first place. That and Deborah's understanding of Rita's need for revenge. 'They're going to be looking for a link between Carpenter and Saville. And if Diller is dead they'll be looking for a link between Carpenter and Saville and Diller.'

'And there clearly is one.'

'And it isn't us,' said Rita.

'It isn't us,' repeated Deborah. 'But it exists, and the police with all their resources are bound to find it, and it will take them in the wrong direction.'

'So when we do the other one…' said Rita.

'The other two,' said Deborah.

'One for now,' said Rita. 'I haven't made my mind up about Jamie Pearson. He wasn't one of the three. He didn't...'

'No,' said Deborah, 'he didn't. But he stood by while the others did.'

'I said I haven't made up my mind, Deborah. He isn't on the list. Not yet.'

'You've still got a soft spot for him. Haven't you?'

'Of course. I only went there in the first place in the hope that he'd be there. I'd seen how he looked at me. I hoped, if I gave him enough chances, he'd speak to me.'

'Instead of which...'

'Yes, yes. So how do we find this Howard Diller?'

'Like this.' And Deborah took the phone she'd extracted from Saville's car and pressed the Recall button.

***

Later, Deborah would find herself thinking about that conversation. "I hate it when you smile like that," Rita had said. Deborah would be happier doing nothing that Rita didn't like, but that wasn't possible. Apart from their disagreement about Jamie Pearson – a disagreement Deborah was determined to win; Jamie Pearson had to die – there were things she couldn't tell Rita because Rita could not be counted on not to blurt them out at the wrong time in the wrong place to the wrong people.

Deborah's escape plans, for example. She knew Rita believed that they could carry on as they were, revenge themselves on a bunch of men who, let's face it, deserved nothing else, and go on living in this house with each other just as they had been doing. Deborah knew better. The police wouldn't let this series of murders rest until they had the killers under lock and key. And that would be even more true when the dead included Jamie Pearson. PC Jamie Pearson. One of theirs. And Deborah had spent time in prison and she wasn't going to experience that again. Not for anyone or anything. Not even for Rita.

And so she had mortgaged the house to the hilt. That hadn't been easy, because she wasn't the house's registered owner and it had taken fancy footwork with documentation, but she'd done it and she'd banked all the money in an account in a name that wasn't hers but for which she had a complete set of documents, even including registration as a nurse. They'd cost her, and it had been money well spent. Most of the people you met in prison you never wanted to see again, but one or two contacts were worth their weight in gold. There was a backpack in a locked cupboard. Deborah called that backpack her flight bag. In it was everything she might need: documents that gave her a new name; debit and credit cards for accounts she'd never used; references and certificates only the most expert would question.

She also had a set for Rita. But Rita knew nothing about this – the time to tell her would be when Deborah knew they had to flee.

Deep down, Deborah was aware that, when that moment came, circumstances might make it impossible to take Rita with her. She blanked that thought. If it happened, it happened; Deborah didn't want to live without Rita, but she wanted to go back to prison even less.

***

As they parked, Susanna was aware that someone was watching them through a window. Before they reached the front door, it had been opened. The woman standing there, watchful, cautious, worried was in her middle years. Susanna thought she'd probably never been what anyone might call beautiful, but life had been good to her. She looked as though laughter would come readily – but she wasn't laughing now.

Susanna held up her warrant card as Ben said, 'Carol, this is Detective Inspector Susanna David. You know who I am.'

'Yes. I know who you are. And I know why you're here. She held up a copy of the Shropshire Star. All it says in here is that Mike has been found dead. What happened?'

Ben said, 'Can we come in, Carol?'

What struck Susanna most about the sitting room they were shown into was its cosy homeliness. Some of the furniture had probably cost serious money when it was new, but that was some time ago. This was a room that had been lived in and enjoyed. The next thing that struck her was that there weren't any photographs and nor were there any pictures.

Carol said, 'Tell me what you're here to say. What happened to Mike?'

Ben knew the woman and Susanna didn't and so she left it to him to break the news of her partner's death. What she made her job was watching the reaction, because the post-mortem had made it clear that Saville must have been held prisoner for some time before he died and yet his absence had not been reported to the police. Her conclusion was that Carol Watts was grieving desperately – but the news had not come as a total surprise. She said, 'Ms Watts. Carol – may I call you Carol? As Ben has told you, we are treating Michael's death as suspicious. Every day that passes gives the person or people responsible more time to hide their tracks, so although I know how much it must hurt, there are questions we have to ask, and we have to ask them quickly.'

Carol nodded. 'Ask what you need to.'

'Thank you, Carol,' said Susanna. 'When did you last see Michael?'

'Five days ago.'

'Did you expect him to be gone that long? Only you don't seem to have reported him missing.'

'Yes. No. I don't know.' She'd been standing

since they came in – now she slumped into a chair and Susanna understood that a resistance had ended. 'Something had been bothering him.'

Susanna nodded. She glanced at Manfredi because he knew the people here and she didn't want him intervening in ways that might be unhelpful. But Manfredi was a policeman before he was anything else and he gave a slight nod that told her he wasn't going to butt in. She said, 'I know this is hurtful, Carol, and after what we've told you I know it won't be something you want to think about, but we can never know in advance what information is going to be helpful. This thing that had been bothering him – do you know what it was?'

It was very clear that a struggle was going on inside Carol's head, but Susanna and Manfredi held their silence. Carol was staring at the floor. Eventually, she said, 'No. But it was about his past.'

'Michael's past? What was there in Michael's past to provoke a row, Carol?'

Her head came up at last, and it was Ben and not Susanna she was looking at. 'That's just it. I don't know.' She had folded her hands together; her fingers seemed to wrestle with each other. 'He said someone was watching him. Someone he'd once known. When I asked who, he didn't answer – not properly. He said it was something from a long time ago.'

'You have no idea what it might be? It's never

come up before?'

'No. Well. How can I tell?' Once again, she was looking at Ben and not at Susanna. 'You knew Mike. You know how he always seemed to be. Generous. Open.'

Ben nodded.

'Sometimes he wasn't quite so open. Sometimes, like in the evening when we'd had dinner and maybe more wine than we should have had, we'd be musing about the past. The way you do. And then I'd get the feeling his mind had drifted to something he didn't want to look at. He'd just close it down. Bring the conversation back to the here and now. Where were we going to go on holiday? Was it time to get the decorator in? After that happened a few times, I knew there was something buried. But what it was, I have no idea.'

Susanna said, 'Did Mike ever mention someone called Terence Carpenter?'

Carol's eyes turned to her. 'That name has been in the news. He was murdered, wasn't he? You think he's connected to Mike?'

'It's too early to say, Carol. This stage in an investigation – all we can do is look for connections. Often, just to eliminate them. But did you ever hear the name before? Did Mike ever talk about him?'

Carol shook her head. 'No. But the stories about Carpenter… They said he was murdered in Batterton. Is that right?'

'Yes. It is. That's where I'm based. Do you know it?'

'No. But it's where Mike grew up, before he went to university and then came here.'

'Did he talk about it much?'

'He didn't talk about it at all. I suggested once that we might go there. Visit his old haunts. He shut me right down. Said he had no good memories of the place and he never wanted to see it again.'

'That's interesting. And he never said why?'

'Never.'

'What about his parents? Might they be able to help?'

'They're both dead. Mike was already an orphan when I met him.'

'I see. Carol, you've been a great help. If you think of anything else we should know, please let Ben know about it. Now, I expect Ben will be arranging a Family Liaison Officer, but is there anyone we can get to come and sit with you?'

CHAPTER 12

Rita wanted to know why Deborah insisted on renting a car to visit Howard Diller – and, if that was how it had to be, why they couldn't hire one locally and instead had first to take the train to a place fifty miles away. Deborah said, 'They have cameras now on all the main roads and a lot of side streets, too. The cameras can read licence plates on cars. Sooner or later, the police are going to be looking at cars that were near where each of these people died. What do you suppose would happen if they found the same car – just one car – in roughly the right place at roughly the right time for each death?'

'They'd want to talk to whoever owned that car.'

'Yes, they would. And they'd find you, and they'd find me, and they'd keep us apart from each other while they asked us both their questions.'

Rita gave one of her shudders. 'I'm sorry. I should have known you'd have a good reason.'

'And, apart from anything else, we need to arrive at Diller's house in a car that looks as though it could belong to the police.'

***

The train was busy enough that they couldn't talk about their plans without the risk of being heard. When they had transferred to the rental car, Rita was free to talk about the things that troubled her.

'What if he has someone there?'

'He won't have. We told him we were coming to talk about the message he'd left on Saville's phone. We don't know yet what that was about, but he does, and he isn't going to want anyone else to hear it being discussed.'

'Do we get to use our warrant cards again?'

'My love, if you want to use your warrant card, use it. It fooled Carpenter, and he's a lawyer, so Diller won't see through it.'

'It's so exciting. Like being on TV. I used to love drama class at school. But suppose he does? See through it?'

'Then I'll blast him with the taser straight away.'

'Suppose the neighbours hear?'

'Isn't that why we looked up his address on Google Earth? He doesn't have any neighbours close enough to hear – if he did, we'd have asked him to meet us somewhere else. In any case, I'm hoping he'll believe us, because I want to record what he says when he thinks he's being interviewed by the police. We can send it to the cops, so they'll know why he and Carpenter and Saville died.'

'You mean, they'll think they know. But they won't really, because we'll have been too clever for them. You will have been too clever for them.' She gave a little shiver that Deborah had learned to recognise as a sign of contentment. 'I'm so lucky I found you.'

'You didn't find me, darling. I found you.'

'And that makes me even luckier.'

'You do realise you're going to have to play with his willy? Just like you did with the other two? We have to make his death look the same as theirs.'

'Oh, I don't mind that. You have got the whisky with you?'

'It's in this bag.'

'You've never told me what it is you put in there.'

'No, I haven't. What you don't know, you can't tell. If you find yourself in a police interview room…'

'But I won't. You're far too clever to let that happen.'

'Even so…'

'Please, Deborah. They always look as though they've died and gone to heaven after you give it to them. And then they do die, of course, and I don't suppose they go anywhere near heaven – but what is it that makes them feel like that?'

'Oh, Rita. It's a mixture of morphine, GHB, MDMA and sildenafil. GHB is what the press calls the date rape drug. MDMA you may know better as ecstasy. Sildenafil is Viagra.'

'Viagra!'

'It probably isn't worth adding that, because it takes a while to work and once they've had a drink we want to get it over with. But I put it in because we need the guy to have a hard on. We want him to die in the very moment of orgasm. And if he can't get it up, how is that going to happen?'

Rita sniggered. 'That certainly hasn't been a problem so far.'

'No. Really, the morphine on its own would probably be enough.' She looked at the satnav. 'We'll be there in ten minutes. Try to get your head in the place it needs to be. You are a detective sergeant, and I'm a detective inspector. We are going to talk to someone who needs our protection. We'll offer it to him, but in return he needs to be completely frank with us.'

'What I'll regret,' said Rita, 'is that we'll have to pop him off straight away. I know we did that with Carpenter, too, because we didn't want to go back to his street.'

'And it will be the same here.'

'Yes. I know. But the best one was Michael Saville. Knowing that he was tied up in that horrible place with no idea whether he was going to live or die. And he'd have known I was involved, because he'd seen me and he must have remembered what he and those animals did to me. Well, we know he did, because he called me Rita and he said he was sorry. That was the best one, Debs. I'd love to do another one where we keep them alive, worrying about what's going to happen, before we pop them.'

'Well, my darling, if the opportunity arises, we'll do it that way again. Maybe with Jamie Pearson.'

'Deborah! You're doing that deliberately. You know I haven't decided about Jamie.'

***

Susanna called DCI Blazeley to say she was on her way and he said he'd hold back the next briefing till she arrived. When she got there, she told Marion to put a new action on HOLMES. 'Check on every birth of a Michael Saville in this area around forty-five years ago. Where did he live, who were his family, is anyone connected to him still alive?' Then she took her seat by Blazeley.

'Right,' said Blazeley. 'Where are we up to? Who wants to go first?'

A DS held up his hand. 'Cyril Bonzer, boss. I checked him out. We all know him, of course, because he's in and out of here all the time.'

'That's a thought,' said Blazeley. 'Nobody from Carpenter and Carpenter told us for almost a week that Terence Carpenter hadn't turned up at work. We now know that he wasn't there because he was dead – but was Bonzer in the station during those four days? Or in court? If he was, why didn't he say anything?'

'I checked that, boss,' said the DS. 'He was the lawyer for the guy you put away for ten years, and he spent almost the whole time in court, running and fetching for defence counsel. Any duty solicitor we needed during that time would have come from another firm.'

'Okay,' said Blazeley. As a chief inspector, he

didn't often find himself in the custody suite or the magistrates' court where a lawyer who was not a barrister could defend his client himself. Cyril Bonser might very well have spent a week in the same courtroom as Blazeley without Blazeley knowing he was there. 'Tell me what you found out about the man.'

'Nothing bad, boss. He doesn't make a secret of being gay but he doesn't shout it from the rooftops, either. He isn't in a settled relationship; lives alone and doesn't have any pets. Drives a three-year-old Skoda and has a one-bedroom flat, so not a big spender. Works out at the gym four or five times a week, doesn't play golf, not known for heavy drinking, neither popular nor unpopular in his own office or with other lawyers in town. More to the point, when he came here he didn't leave behind any unpleasant stories or unfinished business. Never been cautioned, investigated or arrested; his DNA and fingerprints aren't on file because there's never been any occasion to take them. If there's anything fishy about the guy, I've missed it. But probably there isn't.'

'Thank you. Is that it?'

'That's it, boss.'

'So who's next?'

A DC held up her hand. 'I checked Terence Carpenter's lunch last Friday. He did have a tuna sandwich, as the post-mortem suggested. His secretary bought it for him along with a bottle of water. Apparently, that was his choice of lunch three days a week; the other two days he had a bacon roll. She thinks he ate it at about midday.'

Blazeley smiled. 'I don't think I'll ever stop being fascinated by the sheer amount of detail we get into in a murder investigation. Marion, I know you're getting all of this down on HOLMES – what do you see as the biggest action still outstanding?'

'Fingerprints on the photograph, sir?'

'Ah, yes. Who was looking after that?'

Rayyan said, 'I've been coordinating that with scenes of crime and the fingerprint technician. Terence Carpenter's prints were on the photo – in fact, they were all over it as though he'd handled it many times.'

A detective constable said, 'Yes, and we can just imagine what someone like him was doing while he looked at it.'

Blazeley said, 'I don't want to hear words like "someone like him" again, Jez. Rayyan?'

'If we exclude Carpenter's prints, we have three other sets. None of them is a match with anyone on file.'

A sense of disappointment rippled round the room. Blazeley said, 'Look. I just felt the temperature drop in here ten degrees. I know it's disappointing when a lead doesn't immediately take us somewhere but all leads represent progress, even when they turn out to be dead ends. We won't solve this murder by some moment of inspiration. That happens on television, not in real life. What will get us to the killer is step by step hard work and ruling out everything until only one thing is left. All right, it's time to get out there again. Back here this evening, please, to get up-to-date with what we've all been doing. And whoever is looking for Credenza, please redouble your efforts. I'm not suggesting she's become a suspect, but she is certainly a person of interest.' To Susanna he said, 'Can we have a word in my office?'

***

Susanna followed Blazeley into his office. Blazeley said, 'I've been thinking about the press.'

'You want to hold a press conference, sir?'

'If we did have a press conference, it would be held by you. I'm SIO here, Susanna. If it all goes south, I'll be the one carrying the can. But I'll give you as much control as possible, bearing in mind the ultimate accountability is mine. If you're afraid I'm here to steal the limelight, put that out of your mind. I've got enough successful cases in my own career history without horning in on one of yours. I do think, though, it may be a little early to hold a press conference. You might want to hold back on that for a day or two. But two men in that photograph with Rigby Hewitt aren't dead yet. How about releasing their photographs? Someone must know who they are.'

'I think you're right, sir. I'll ask the press office to get them out there.'

'Agreed. You have my complete support in doing that. And I'll make a policy book entry to record that support.'

CHAPTER 13

Someone was watching their arrival through the front window. 'Good,' said Deborah. 'He's nervous. Let's keep him that way. Get your notebook out – let's make sure we look official.'

Howard Diller did indeed look nervous. He led the way into a large kitchen that was equipped like something out of a TV cooking special. 'Do you mind if we talk in here?'

Rita took out her notebook and Deborah put on the table a small digital recorder. They had bought both items the previous day for just this purpose. Diller said, 'What's that for?'

Deborah said, 'It's just to make sure that we understand later exactly what you're going to tell us, Mr Diller. May I call you Howard? You're not under arrest, and if that ever changes you will receive a formal warning and be invited to have a lawyer with you. But at the moment, all we know is that you suggested to Michael Saville that you and he had information relating to Terence Carpenter that you should take to the police. Terence Carpenter was murdered and when you made the call to Michael Saville you knew that. Now Michael Saville is also dead. So, Howard – what is it you felt we should know?'

Diller was shaking. He looked pale. He said, 'Saville? Dead?'

'You didn't know? It will be all over the papers

tomorrow.'

'I wonder if I should have a lawyer with me now?'

Deborah said, 'That's entirely your decision, Howard. Are you going to admit to a criminal offence?'

'Yes. No. I don't know.'

'I see. Let's try to approach this in general terms. If you were going to admit to a criminal offence, what would the offence be?'

Diller looked at the floor. His voice when he spoke was scarcely above a whisper. He said, 'Rape. Of a young man.'

'I see. Well, Howard, I'm not going to try to mislead you – that is a serious offence and it could very well carry a prison sentence. Though I'd expect the judge to go easy on you because you had sought us out to tell us about it. But when did this happen?'

'Seventeen years ago.'

'Ah. Then you have nothing to worry about, and there's nothing we could do even if we wanted to. Have you heard of the statute of limitations, Howard?'

'I… No.'

To Rita, watching this was a reminder of how much she loved Deborah and how much she owed her. She, Rita, knew nothing about the statute of limitations, and she was pretty sure Deborah knew no more than she did – and yet to get Howard Diller to unburden himself she was going to talk about it as though she did.

Deborah said, 'The statute of limitations lays down how long the police have to bring a prosecution. For some minor crimes, it isn't long at all – if you steal a Snickers bar from your local corner shop we have to charge you within an absolute maximum of six months or we can't charge you at all. On the other hand, if you commit murder, there is no limitation – we can still charge you fifty years after the event if that's when we get the evidence we need. You've probably heard about cases like that – in the police, we call them cold cases. At the time the murder was committed, we had a good idea who did it but we didn't have the evidence to prove it. Then along comes DNA and, suddenly, we do.'

Rita's eyes were fixed on Diller. He was nodding, as if to say, "Yes – I have heard about cases like that." She realised that everything was going to be fine: Diller had accepted them both at face value and he was being taken in completely by Deborah's confiding manner. Deborah was setting him up for the drop, and he was walking willingly into it. With difficulty, she resisted an urge to hug Deborah – if anything would put the cat among the pigeons, it was that.

Deborah said, 'For the offence you mention, the limitation is set at seven years. So, you see, Howard, you have nothing to worry about. You will be admitting to something we can't charge you for. Now, why don't you get it off your chest?'

***

Jamie Pearson was struggling with a dilemma. Of course, he'd remembered the name of Terence Carpenter. Carpenter was not just a lawyer he saw regularly in the custody suite and occasionally in court; Carpenter had been one of those who had attacked Rita on that dreadful day. But that was just one person. It meant nothing. The addition of Michael Saville changed that. Because Michael Saville had been another of Rita's attackers.

Coincidence? Well, it certainly could be. In fact, it almost certainly was. But Jamie was a policeman and policemen are taught that coincidences should be viewed with suspicion until it is proved that coincidence is all they are. The conclusion was obvious: he should tell DI David or DCI Blazeley that the two dead men in the case they were investigating were connected by a twenty-year-old attack on a young woman – really, a girl.

And if he should do that, he would do it. Not today, because today was his day off and he was sitting by a river, fishing. The sun was shining; he had with him a flask of coffee, two bottles of water, a pork pie, a packet of crisps and some sandwiches; he felt no urge to involve himself in work. And it wasn't as though he was part of the investigation; Jamie was a uniformed officer and not a detective and, while he had been one of the two who answered the control room call and found Terence Carpenter's body, he hadn't been assigned to the investigation. Not admitting his involvement and getting himself removed from the case would not jeopardise any prosecution because he wasn't on the case in the first place. Tomorrow would be soon enough.

He stopped thinking about it and went back to watching the float on his fishing line. It seemed to Jamie that sitting quietly watching his float was a large part of what he did when he was fishing. And that was okay; if he'd wanted a leisure activity filled with action and talking to people, he'd have joined a tennis club.

But, beneath the sunshine-fuelled lethargy, thinking was still going on. Michael Saville and Terence Carpenter – what had brought them together that appalling day? From what he remembered, which admittedly wasn't much, they weren't close friends. Carpenter was only there because it was the school holidays. Normally, he'd have been more than a hundred miles away at his expensive public school. And while it wasn't the sort of thing people their age talked about at that time, he thought the general assumption about Carpenter was that he'd have been more interested in a boy than a girl. An assumption Jamie now knew would have been correct. And yet, Carpenter had been the most vicious and violent of the three rapists, and the leader – without him driving it, Jamie didn't think it would have happened. As for Saville and the third one, Ralph Townsend, Jamie had thought then and still thought now that their hearts hadn't really been in it. What they'd really wanted was a barney with the local boys. To this day, he still wished he'd given it to them.

CHAPTER 14

Howard Diller was avoiding looking at either of them. His head was bowed, he spoke in a voice laden with regret, and his hands were wrapped tight around each other. He said, 'The boy's name was Rigby Hewitt. We knew him. We had all known him.'

Deborah said, 'Are you using that word in the biblical sense, Howard?' When Diller nodded, she said, 'For the tape, please, Howard – this isn't going to be used in court because, as we've already discussed, you can't be prosecuted for an offence of this type that happened so long ago, but we still need to hear your answers. When you say, "We had all known him," did you mean…'

'Yes!' A spark of fury came into Diller's eyes as he looked up. 'Yes, that's exactly what I mean. He was just like us. But younger.'

'Just like you?'

'Gay. Queer. A homo. There was a scene, and we were part of it, and so was he.'

'Then I don't understand, Howard,' said Deborah. 'You used the word "rape," which suggests he wasn't willing.'

'Carpenter had brought him along. I think Rigby believed it was to be just the two of them. The way Carpenter had set it up, that was how it started – just him and the boy.'

'And at that point, Rigby was cooperating?'

'Cooperating? He was enjoying himself. But then the rest of us came in, and he realised what we had in mind, and he objected.'

'I want to be sure I understand this, Howard – you had planned all this in advance?'

'Yes, we had. Carpenter said the boy was getting above himself and needed to be taught a lesson.'

'So when he objected…'

'We took no notice.'

'I see. Well, Howard, that's not a very elevating story, is it? And at the end?'

'What do you mean, at the end?'

'It seems a fairly simple question to me, Howard. When you were all done, at which point I imagine this boy's arse must have been like the inside of a paperhanger's bucket, what happened to him?'

Diller looked shocked. 'Well, we didn't kill him, if that's what you're thinking. We gave him some money and he went home.'

'You gave him some money?'

'That's what we always did. He was a bit of a tart, if you want to know. But I was revolted by what we'd done. I'd never had anyone by force before that, and I never have since. Force was Carpenter's default approach. With men or women. I broke with that crowd shortly afterwards.'

'Revolted,' said Deborah. 'You were revolted. Yes, I can understand that. But you weren't revolted enough not to do it when it was your turn?'

When Diller shook his head, Deborah said, 'For the tape, please, Howard,' and Diller said, 'I did it.'

'Well,' said Deborah. 'Someone seems to be taking revenge on the four of you. There are only two of you left – you and the person whose name you haven't yet given to us. And we need you to do that, Howard, because whatever we may feel about what you've done it's our job to protect you. And we also need to protect him. In order to do which, we need to know his name.' She switched off the tape recorder. 'So who is he, Howard?'

***

Barney Carpenter had given Nicola the name of the cleaning company used by Barney, by the partnership, and by Terence Carpenter. The cleaning company had given her the name of Amara Hossain. She was not happy to be interviewed. 'I promised not to say anything.'

This was not the response Nicola had expected. 'About what, Amara?'

'They made a deal. My brother and Mr Carpenter. Mr Carpenter paid some money and my brother promised I wouldn't say anything. Not to the police, not to anyone.'

'Amara, Mr Carpenter is dead. So any deal you made with him, you can now forget. We are trying to find out who killed him, and what you have to tell us may help. Now, what was it you promised not to say anything about?'

'You want to know who killed him? Maybe it was someone whose family cared more about what he did to them than about money. Maybe it was someone whose brother had a sense of honour.'

A hint of what this might be about had entered Nicola's mind. 'Do you think it would help if we asked your brother to join us?'

'No! I did not come to England to still be in Jordan. I did not make this journey so that my brother could still decide what was right for me.'

'How much money did Mr Carpenter pay for your silence, Amara?'

The woman looked furious. 'I do not know. He gave it to my brother. My brother has it. How much it was, he never told me. All he told me was that I could not say anything.'

'Amara, if you had no money, you made no deal. Apart from which, when two parties make a deal and one of them dies, the deal is over. That is the law in Britain.'

'That is the law?'

'That is the law. Now, I need to know: if Mr Carpenter had not paid money to your brother, what might you have told the police about?'

Amara was silent, but Nicola could see from her face that she was thinking, and she kept her own silence. Then Amara said, 'He attacked me.'

'Mr Carpenter attacked you? Hit you? Was he angry?'

'He looked in a rage. His face was so red it was almost black. I thought he was going to kill me.'

'What was it that made him so angry?'

'What do you think? What is it ever that makes a man angry with a woman?'

Now, there was something for Nicola to think about. If Amara meant what she seemed to mean, then that might make many men angry with a woman, but she would not have expected Terence Carpenter to be one of them. She said, 'Amara, we are talking about Mr Carpenter? Mr Terence Carpenter? The man who lived until recently at 36 Parkside Ave?'

'Yes! Him! Who else? That is who they told me you wanted to know about.'

'I see. Amara, everything we know about Terence Carpenter says that he isn't going to be interested in a woman in that way.'

'Hah! Then you do not know enough about him.'

'You're sure about this? I mean, for example, did he ask for… For services of that kind?'

'Ask? ASK? No, he did not ask – he threw himself on me. And some of the words he was using – I have been in this country long enough now to have heard the sort of language people use. I do not hear many say things like that.'

'But you escaped?'

There was a long silence. Then, 'No. I did not escape. And when I got home, my brother and my father knew what had happened.'

'Because you were upset?'

'Yes, yes, because of that – but also because my clothes were torn and I had a black eye. I said we must go to the police. But they…'

'Your father and your brother?'

'Yes, them – they told me to take a shower, get changed and say nothing. My brother said, if anyone knew what had happened to me, no-one would marry me. And I said, if what I had just been through was what happened in marriage, I would rather be single. My father slapped me and called me… You don't need to know what he called me. Then my brother went to see your Mr Carpenter. And when he came back he said Carpenter had paid money and I was to say nothing to anyone. I said I would not go back there and my brother said I had to, that that was part of the agreement, but that nothing like what had happened would happen again.'

'And it hasn't?'

'No, it hasn't. And now it can't because the man who attacked me is dead. And if you want me to say I'm sorry he's dead, you will wait a very long time.'

***

The call from Rigby Hewitt took Susanna by surprise. And Rigby Hewitt was not a happy man. 'Why did you speak to my agent? I haven't been in England for years. I'm a Canadian citizen now. I've tried to put the whole of that time out of my mind. A few months ago, my agent got me the offer of a part in a movie, some of which was going to be shot in London, and I turned it down. The money was good, the part was good – I just didn't want to be back there. It didn't do my relationship with my agent any good at all. And then you come, disturbing things so badly I have to take a flight at my own expense to a place with wi-fi so I can speak to you. What do you want?'

'We are investigating two murders, Mr Hewitt. The first was Terence Carpenter and the second was Michael Saville. I believe you knew both of them.'

There was the hesitation that policemen expect when someone learns that someone else has died. And then, 'Yes. I did. And I'm not sorry either of them is dead. But I didn't kill them and I have no idea who did.'

'Would you mind telling me how you came to know them?'

'I suspect you know, or you wouldn't be asking.'

Susanna knew a conversation like this could go back-and-forth for a long time and that the end of it might be for Rigby Hewitt to get back on a plane and return to his film set. She said, 'If you have wi-fi where you are, are you able to receive an email without anyone else seeing it?'

'Send it by WhatsApp. It's more secure that way. Use this phone number I'm speaking to you from – it's my cell phone.'

Susanna pulled up the picture of the person they thought was Rigby Hewitt and the three men that Nicola had brought from Terence Carpenter's safe and sent it, adding the question, "Is this you?"

Moments later, Hewitt was back on the phone. 'Yes, that's me. So you did know how I came to know Carpenter and Saville. As I suggested.'

'Mr Hewitt – Rigby – would you mind telling me who the other man is?'

'Why?'

'Two of those three men are dead. We'd like to prevent the other one meeting the same fate.'

'Why on earth should he?'

'Don't you think it's a remarkable coincidence that two out of those three men have been murdered?'

'No, I don't, and I'll tell you why. Your reasoning is based on the assumption that Carpenter and Saville were murdered for revenge. And the only person who might have wanted revenge is me. And I didn't kill them.'

'I'd be really grateful if you would give me the man's name.'

'I'm sorry. My mind has gone blank. I can't remember who he was. That part of my life is a closed book now. I don't lead that life any longer.'

'Mr Hewitt, if we bring someone to trial for having sex with a minor, we'll need you to give evidence.'

'Not a chance. Not a fucking prayer.' And the phone went dead.

***

If Rigby Hewitt was unwilling to tell Susanna who the other man in the photograph was, Howard Diller was quite the opposite. He seemed, if anything, relieved to have given up the name of the fourth person involved when Hewitt had been raped. And Deborah was delighted to have got it out of him – though she'd made sure by turning off the tape recorder that it would not be passed on to the police when she sent them the recording.

'What happens now?' asked Diller.

'Well,' said Deborah, 'I think after that you deserve a little treat. Don't you agree, Sergeant?' She had to direct a very firm look at Rita before Rita understood that that question was addressed to her.

'Oh, yes,' said Rita. 'You've been very helpful, Howard.' It was only with an effort that she avoided going on to tell him what a good boy he'd been. She had felt so proud of Deborah as she watched her manipulating Diller and turning him to her will.

Deborah said, 'Where do you keep your glasses?'

'Glasses?'

'You know. For drinking out of.'

'Oh.' He pointed at one of the wall cupboards. 'There.' Deborah opened a cupboard, took out a glass and took her whisky bottle out of her bag. Diller said, 'Only one glass? Aren't you going to join me?'

'We'd love to,' said Deborah, 'but we have to drive when we leave here. And it isn't really a treat, Howard. What the police have learned over the years is that, when someone has gone through the kind of interrogation you've just gone through, they suffer from shock. It isn't something we talk about, but we put something into this whisky that helps you overcome the shock.' She poured whisky into the glass and handed it to him. 'There you are. Drink up.'

CHAPTER 15

Nicola was wondering whether she could squeeze in a quick sandwich and coffee for lunch. In the end, she decided she had better delay any break until she'd completed the task she'd been assigned of checking for the birth of a Michael Saville at roughly the right time. It didn't take long. Susanna was not at her desk and so Nicola legged it to the canteen where she refuelled on coffee, a bottle of water and a cheese and tomato sandwich. When she got back to the incident room, Susanna was there to hear what Nicola had discovered. 'You're telling me that Michael Saville's parents are still alive and still living in this town?'

'That's what the records say, boss.'

'Well done, Nicola.' To Marion Trimble she said, 'Put this on HOLMES, will you? Nicola and I are going to interview the supposedly deceased parents of the definitely deceased Michael Saville. Come on, Nic – you can drive.'

The Savilles lived in a pebble-dashed semi-detached house in a street that was quiet because it was a cul-de-sac. Nobody went through here on their way to somewhere else – you either came because this was where you wanted to be, or you didn't come. Susanna and Nicola held up their warrant cards and Susanna said, 'Mrs Saville?' When the woman had nodded, Susanna said, 'I'm Detective Inspector Susanna David and this is

Detective Constable Nicola Hayward.'

More often than not, speaking those words brought out apprehension if not actually fear. That was not Mrs Saville's response. She simply looked at them, eyebrows raised, waiting for them to explain why they were there. When Susanna said, 'May we come in?' Mrs Saville stepped back and ushered them into the hall and then into a sitting room where a man of about Mrs Saville's age looked up from the television on which he was watching cricket. 'It's the police, darling,' said Mrs Saville. Her husband's response was the same as hers had been – interested, slightly puzzled, but not concerned.

Susanna went through the warrant card introductions again. Then she said, 'We're here about your son.'

Mrs Saville's hand went to her mouth. 'Donald? What's happened to him?'

'Not Donald, Mrs Saville,' said Susanna. 'I'm afraid I didn't know you had another son.'

Now it was Mr Saville's turn to speak and when he did it was with more than a touch of hostility. 'We don't,' he said. 'We have only one son and that is Donald. We did have a second son, but he ceased to be a child of ours a long time ago. We don't speak of him and we don't welcome being reminded that he exists somewhere. Now, if that's all…'

Susanna fought down an urge to laugh. 'I'm afraid it can't be all, Mr Saville. Michael Saville is dead and my job is to find out why.'

'Dead?' echoed Mrs Saville, her voice wavering. 'But what… How…?'

'We are treating the death as suspicious,' said Susanna.

'By suspicious,' said Mr Saville, 'you mean he was murdered. Say what you mean, woman. There's too much namby-pamby obfuscation nowadays. I'm surprised you said the boy was dead and didn't say he'd passed on. In any case, it's no concern of ours. I expect he deserved it.'

Susanna said, 'Mr Saville, would you mind telling me what caused you to fall out so comprehensively with Michael?'

'Yes. I would mind. My wife and I have committed no crime and we have no interest in anyone else's wrongdoings. What are you going to do – arrest us? For what?'

'It is an offence, Mr Saville, to obstruct the police in the execution of their duties.'

Saville laughed. It astounded Susanna that anyone should laugh when brought news of the murder of his son, but that's what he did. He held out both arms, wrists together. 'I'm not telling you anything. If you think that amounts to obstruction, arrest me. If you're not going to arrest me, bugger off out of my house and leave me to watch the cricket in peace.'

Susanna knew she should be cross about Saville's attitude. What she in fact felt was a mixture of frustration and admiration. She really did need to know what had caused the breach between Saville and his parents, but she wasn't going to learn the answer here. She took out a card and handed it to Mrs Saville. 'If, when you've thought a little more about whether the person who murdered Michael Saville should get away with it, you feel there is anything more we should know, please call me.'

Saville held out his hand and his wife placed Susanna's card in it. Without even glancing at what was written there, Saville tore it into small pieces and dropped them into the empty fireplace. Mrs Saville gave an embarrassed giggle, and Susanna and Nicola showed themselves out.

***

'I might as well have restricted it to the morphine,' said Deborah. 'That's what works so fast. I mean, look at him. It's the same sort of response as we get from patients when we are managing their pain in the last stages. Anyway, do we need to bother getting him upstairs to bed? This is a nice big kitchen and a nice big kitchen table. Why don't we hoist him up and do him here? You get his legs and I'll take his arms.'

All of that was simply background noise in Howard Diller's head. He was vaguely aware that he was being lifted up and laid flat. He knew at some level of consciousness that his clothes were being removed, but he simply didn't care why. It was amazing to think that these two lovely, lovely

133

ladies were from the police. Diller had never thought of kindness when he thought about the police – they were people to avoid if you could. But the younger one – was she the sergeant? He thought that's how she'd been introduced – was so gentle as she slipped his Comfort Republic underpants down his legs and off. "Buy me – your balls will thank you" the advert had said and it had been right – his balls had thanked him. And now they were thanking him even more as the sergeant's hand brought him towards his climax. Amazing to think that he could get this amount of pleasure from a woman – he wished he'd known that before. A lot of things in his life might have been different.

And then the heavenly rush was upon him and he felt his hips lifting from the table and the unimaginable, indescribable leap over the waterfall began.

At which point, Deborah took the long cable tie from her pocket and ended Howard Diller's time on earth.

***

When they were driving back to the place from which they had rented the car, Rita said, 'Those patients that you give the morphine to. You'll have been giving them less than usual recently?'

'Some of them,' said Deborah. 'Otherwise, I wouldn't have had enough for our shenanigans. Morphine is carefully controlled in the hospital. If

134

I just helped myself, the figures wouldn't balance and someone would notice.'

'It seems a little unfair on the poor patients.'

'Yes, I suppose it does. In a perfect world, we could deal with your rapists without the patients going short. Sadly, this is not a perfect world.'

'How do you know how much morphine to give them?'

'The amount needed is carefully worked out according to weight and various other things. And then it's approved by a doctor. We're encouraged to err on the side of caution – to give a little less and not a little more. You have to be careful – one of those ampoules I have at home would kill even a healthy young person like you in two minutes or so. The idea is to make the patient free of pain but to allow nature to take its course.'

'Honestly, Deborah, I don't know how you can be so caring about your patients and so murderous towards the victims. But, really, it was the victims I was talking about.'

'Oh, the victims. First time I mixed the drugs into the whisky, I added two whole ampoules. You'll notice I pour a healthy glass full – there's enough morphine in that amount to make the victim off his head and totally unaware of what's going on without any danger of killing him before we want him to die. And I do care about the patients, but not only about them.'

'I know.' Rita pressed her back into the car seat, squirming with happiness. She reached over and placed a hand on Deborah's thigh. 'You care about me, too.'

'I care about you more than anything. That's why I do this.'

'I know,' said Rita. 'And you'll get your reward when we get home.'

'Promises, promises. You sexy beast.'

'It's a pity I can't work on this drawing on the train home.'

'Well, you can't, so put it right out of your mind. Imagine if another passenger looked at what you were drawing.'

'They wouldn't know the drawing was real. They'd just think I had a nasty imagination.'

'Rita. Do not do it. Wait until tomorrow.'

Deborah liked those drawings Rita did of the people they killed. The men looked so peaceful when she had ended it all for them. There was another picture Deborah would dearly love to make it possible for Rita to draw. That would be the death of Mavis Ritzig. Deborah had never mentioned Mavis Ritzig to Rita and probably never would. She'd have loved to be responsible for Mavis's death in the way she was for Howard Diller, the man they had just launched into eternity. It couldn't happen, because Deborah had no idea where Mavis was now and no idea how to find her. But of one thing she was sure. If she ever did find Mavis Ritzig, and manufacture an opportunity to end that repellent woman's life, Mavis would not look afterwards as though she was at peace.

Deborah had listened to Rita talking about what those three men had done to her and, yes, they deserved to die for it. Was it any worse than what Mavis Ritzig had organised other female prisoners to do to Deborah? Deborah didn't think so.

CHAPTER 16

Bazza Humphreys was wild with fury. Postmen get to work in the morning before the newspapers are on the street and so he hadn't seen the photographs plastered all over them, saying, "Do you know these men?" When he started his round, he'd noticed one or two people looking at him a little oddly. Eventually, someone showed him the paper. One of the pictures was him. It had been taken fifteen years earlier and he was thirty-four now and not nineteen anymore, so he could get away with saying, "Yes, it's a strong resemblance, but it isn't me." And that's what he had done and what he intended to go on doing.

But Mrs Carrick had as good as made it clear that she didn't believe him. She'd always been a nuisance – if mail she was expecting didn't arrive, she demanded to know where it was as if its lateness was his fault. And that time she ordered something from America and when it arrived he had to ask her for the balance of postage, you'd have thought he was robbing her. And now she said, even after he'd told her it wasn't him in the photograph, she was going to ring the paper and tell them where he was. 'There might be a reward,' she said.

He'd like to wring her neck. He couldn't be sure where this photograph had come from, but it wasn't someone with his best interests at heart. He wondered what had happened to Rigby Hewitt. Nothing good, he could be sure of that.

So he left Mrs Carrick with something so close to an oath that she said she was going to call his bosses at the post office and complain about him. At least that would be better than calling the newspaper.

As he went on with his deliveries, he thought a bit more about how the photograph had come into the hands of the police. Because the police were behind this – he knew that, even if the paper didn't say it outright. Carpenter was dead. That had been in the papers, and on the television, too. Carpenter was dead "in suspicious circumstances." And Carpenter had almost certainly had a copy of that photograph. If it was the one Bazza was certain it was, Carpenter had been the star – the man in the saddle – the one with his manhood in a place where straight society believed someone's manhood should not be.

Quite apart from which, wouldn't anyone still alive be running a huge risk by taking that photograph to the cops? They'd been committing a criminal offence, when all was said and done. Yes, the kid had been willing, but he'd been under the age of consent. Bazza thought about the three of them who remained. Carpenter might have sufficient courage – but Carpenter was dead. He didn't see either of the others as likely to take that kind of chance.

Suppose the cops, when they investigated

Carpenter's "suspicious" death, had found that photograph? And suppose they now wanted to find everyone else in it? Wasn't that the most likely way they'd come by the picture?

And Bazza went on working himself up over all the possible scenarios for disaster inherent in that idea, until he arrived at the house of Mrs Carrick's rival for the title of worst delivery on the round. Sydney Borzoi was waiting for him, newspaper in hand and gloating expression on his face. Bazza held up a hand. 'Don't you start. I've had enough already. Yes, it looks like me – but it isn't.'

'Don't talk rubbish,' said Borzoi. 'It's you to the life.'

And Bazza hit him.

Satisfying as it was to see the blood spouting through the hand Borzoi clapped over his nose, Bazza felt unfulfilled as he went on with his deliveries. People had no right to put his photograph in the papers. Leaving aside the doubts it was going to raise about him, with colleagues and management as well as the public, he did his best to damp down fears about what could happen. Bazza had only been nineteen, it was fifteen years ago, nothing like that had happened since and it was exactly the sort of thing a court would hand out a suspended sentence for.

If his head hadn't been full of these worries, maybe he'd have handled it differently when he got back to the sorting office at the end of his delivery round and found the police waiting to discuss Borzoi's bloody nose. When the constable, who had checked and knew that Bazza had never in his life been in any trouble with the law, said that he felt in this case there was no need for further action and he was going to give Bazza a caution, Bazza blew his top. 'No! You can stick your caution up your arse! Charge me or bugger off!' He said that in every confidence that the cop wouldn't want to waste time booking someone for a minor charge like giving someone a bloody nose. He had made a mistake.

The cop looked very displeased. Bazza had expected him to leave. If the cops thought a caution was enough, why would they bother with a charge? Everybody knew cops were bone idle, and arresting someone meant paperwork to complete. But that isn't what happened. With a disgruntled expression, the cop said, 'Very well, sir. I'm arresting you on suspicion of assault causing actual bodily harm. You do not have to say anything, but it may harm your defence if you do not mention when questioned something which you later rely on in court. Anything you do say may be given in evidence. Get into the car, please.'

Bazza knew he'd made a mistake. Deep down, he knew the only sensible response was to step back, apologise for being so hot-headed, explain what a hard morning he'd had, and agree to be cautioned. If he'd done that, chances were the cop would have accepted the apology and cautioned him – the cop didn't want to have to go to the station any more than Bazza did. But Bazza couldn't quite bring himself to back down and, when the cop presented him to the custody sergeant and explained why he had been arrested, and then the custody sergeant said they were going to take his fingerprints and a DNA sample, it was too late. DNA! What did they have from that time with Rigby Hewitt? He'd heard about cold cases, and how DNA could get people found guilty decades after they thought they'd got away with it. He'd left after banging Hewitt. He didn't know what had happened to him, but suppose Carpenter had done away with him? He was quite capable of it; Terence Carpenter was the single most unpleasant person Bazza had ever met, not excluding himself. And Bazza had never heard anything about Rigby Hewitt after that day. If the body had just been found, was it possible that DNA had lingered? It was a chance not worth taking. He said, 'Look. I'm sorry. It's my fault – I was angry. Nothing to do with you. I accept your caution.'

The custody sergeant looked at the constable, eyebrow raised. If he chose to substitute a caution for an arrest, she would accept that. Anything that avoided another body in custody was a bonus – even if, as in this case, they were likely to bail the guy immediately they completed the documentation and fingerprinting. But the constable was now as furious as Bazza. 'No, you don't,' he said. 'You've given me too much trouble. You're under arrest.'

The custody sergeant sighed and said, 'Empty your pockets, please, sir.'

As it turned out, when the formalities had been completed, Bazza was not released on bail. He was asked to take a seat in a cell and listened with a sinking heart to the sound of the door being locked. The custody sergeant phoned Susanna. 'Ma'am, we've just fingerprinted a man called Barry Humphreys. He goes by the name of Bazza.'

'Do I know him?' said Susanna.

'Possibly not,' said the sergeant. 'But I think you should take a look at him. His face is the spit of one of the photographs in the newspapers today.'

***

After a series of foolish decisions, Bazza at least had the sense to say yes when asked if he wanted a duty solicitor. Cyril Bonser was on the rota for that day and spent thirty minutes in a specially adapted interview room in the custody suite talking to him about the best way to handle the interviews. The gaydar Bonser had referred to when talking to Gareth Forester was at work again; both men knew very quickly that they shared at least one interest. Cyril said, 'Have you ever been interviewed by the police?'

Bazza shook his head. 'Never.'

'Well, it isn't like you may have seen on television. When you were arrested, you were cautioned. Do you remember the words whoever arrested you used?'

Bazza shrugged. 'Who listens at a time like that?'

'Well, you should have. I can promise you that the officer who arrested you said, "You do not have to say anything. But it may harm your defence if you do not mention when questioned something which you later rely on in court. Anything you do say may be given in evidence." That's PACE. The Police and Criminal Evidence Act. And what the interview will be about is trying to get you to say things that they can prove aren't true, or trying to get you not to say things that you will then want to use in court. So let's talk about what you're going to be charged with. Because I suspect that, when the interview comes to an end, you will be charged. The police are supposed to tell me all the reasons they are holding you. They almost never do that. But they have to tell me something, and what they've said so far is that they have a photograph of you engaged in an illegal act involving the rape of a young man called Rigby Hewitt. Did you rape Rigby Hewitt?'

'Rape? He was gagging for it.'

'How old was he?'

'Fifteen.'

'Then it was rape, however willing he was. My job is to advise you how to answer questions and my advice is: when they ask you to confirm that you had intercourse with that boy, admit that you

144

did. Don't say anything else – don't answer any more questions unless I say you can.'

'Listen, this was all a hell of a long time ago. Can they still bring it up?'

'Yes, they can. The statute of limitations in this country only applies to minor, summary criminal offences of a kind dealt with by magistrates. There's no limitation on any offence that would be tried by a judge. If they can prove you did it, you can be tried, whenever it happened. What happened to the minor?'

'I've no idea.'

'Well, we'd better hope he is alive and well. Or, if he isn't, that we can prove his death had nothing to do with you. Okay. That's enough preparation. I'll tell the custody sergeant we're ready for you to be interviewed.'

They were then left for half an hour with only a silent uniformed constable for company. 'Don't let it get to you,' said Cyril. 'This is what they think of as a softening up process. And bear in mind that this interview will be watched. They don't have two-way mirrors – that's strictly for books and television – but they will have monitors and they will be listening and watching.'

Cyril was probably right about the softening up process, but DC Gareth Forester did need to talk to his interviewing colleague, DC Sally Barnes, about how they were going to handle the interview – a conversation that Susanna sat in on. When Gareth and Sally left, Susanna went with DCI

Blazeley to watch on monitors as Gareth and Sally entered the interview room and the uniformed constable left. Gareth started the recording machine, after which all four people present stated their names and Sally dictated the date and the time. Gareth said, 'Mr Humphries. May I call you Barry?'

'No one else does,' said Bazza. 'But feel free. You're in charge.'

CHAPTER 17

Jamie Pearson's fishing day had not brought the level of calm he had hoped for. He was on patrol with PC Theresa McErlane and Theresa, who was driving, had just about had enough. She said, 'What the hell is the matter with you today? You can't stop fidgeting, you don't give a straight answer to a question and you look as though you're waiting for professional standards to arrest you. I've had two hours of this; I can't take it for the rest of the shift. Either tell me what's troubling you or get yourself moved to another car.'

Jamie, who was so absorbed in his own worries that he had had no idea he was getting on his partner's nerves, looked up. 'I'm sorry. I didn't know I was letting it show.'

'Well,' said Theresa, 'at least that's confirmation there's something to let show. So what is it?'

'Terence Carpenter.'

'The lawyer who was topped? What about him?'

'I knew him.'

'We all knew him. We saw him in the station. He was in and out like a fiddler's elbow.'

'No. Before that. I knew him when I was young. Not well – his father had pots of money and Carpenter went to a very good school. Harrow, I think. As a boarder. And he was older than me. But when he was home for holidays, he'd hang out with some of the older guys I knew.'

'Jamie, you can't go into your shell just because someone you once knew is dead. We all used to know someone who is now dead.'

'Michael Saville. I knew him, too. Knew him better than I knew Carpenter, because he was a couple of years above me at school.'

'Oh. But look – that's still just coincidence. As long as you weren't actually involved in something serious that they were also involved in.'

'That's just the point, Theresa. I was. Well, not involved, exactly – but I was there.'

'Oh, shit. Have you told anyone?'

'No. And that's what's worrying me. Should I tell? '

'Of course you should. Even if what happened when you were there is nothing to do with why they died, you still need to let MCIT know. It's for them to decide what's relevant – not you.'

'That's what I keep telling myself. But it isn't that simple. I don't come out of that story looking at all good.'

Theresa resisted with difficulty the urge she had to wrap her arms around Jamie and hug him. It was an urge she'd had before and it made her cross. Everyone knew getting involved with a colleague was a mistake. Especially in the police. So why couldn't these urges when they came be aimed at someone else? A grocer, perhaps. That way there'd always be fresh fruit to eat, and she wouldn't get home to realise she'd forgotten yet again to buy vegetables for dinner. Or a long-distance lorry driver, so she'd have time on her own. 'Oh, Jamie. I'm sorry I shouted at you. I had no idea you were going through something like this. You want to tell me about it?'

***

The crime scene manager from the Carpenter murder slipped into the room where Susanna David and Bill Blazeley were about to watch the Bazza Humphries interview. 'We've got the DNA results. The first thing you need to know is that the semen on Terence Carpenter's stomach was his own. The second is that we found someone else's DNA on Carpenter's penis. It's reasonable to suppose that that may be the DNA of the person who masturbated Carpenter as he died, though we can't be certain and, in any case, we can't identify that person because their DNA is not on file. I can tell you, though, that the masturbator was female.'

'Thank you, Charlie. Too early for the toxicology reports, I suppose?'

''Fraid so. I'll try to get them moved up the queue, but you know how it is.'

'Well, thanks for this, anyway. I'm going to let Gareth and Sally know – it will help them in the interview.' She entered the details into her phone and texted it to Gareth. She always laughed when she watched a cop show on television and saw an officer's dramatic interruption of an interview.

149

You might interrupt an interview to tell the people in the room that the building was on fire. No other reason would make you do it.

***

'Barry,' said Gareth. 'Did you know Terence Carpenter?'

'Yes,' said Bazza.

'How did you know him?'

'When we were young... He was away during the term but he'd come home for holidays and we'd see him.'

'We?'

'Me and... Some others.'

'I see. Did you have any contact with Terence Carpenter in more recent years?'

'I didn't see him to talk to for more than ten years.'

'Not to talk to... All right. But you saw him? From time to time?'

Bazza's face tightened. 'We had a number of illnesses at work – a little epidemic – and those of us who didn't catch it had to cover for other people. I found myself delivering mail to him. Do you know what kind of car he drove?'

'I don't get the connection, Barry,' said Gareth who, in fact, got it only too well. 'Do you mean you felt jealous?'

Bazza settled back in his seat, realising that he was giving too much away. He said, 'I thought he was doing pretty well.'

'Pretty well?'

'Better than me!'

'Yes. I see. But other than that… You haven't seen him?'

Bazza shook his head. 'No. Other than that, I haven't seen him.'

Gareth placed in front of Bazza an evidence bag containing the photograph of three men and Rigby Hewitt. He said for the benefit of the tape, 'I'm showing Mr Humphries a photograph registered as Exhibit NH/1.' He pointed at one of the three. 'Is that you, Barry?'

'Yes,' Bazza said, 'that's me.'

'And the boy – what was his name?'

'Rigby Hewitt.' Bazza had expected this interview to be painful. In fact, it was the easiest thing in the world. He was being asked questions and he was answering them. Answering truthfully. It could go that way when you knew you had no choice.

'How old was Rigby Hewitt when that photograph was taken, Barry? And how old were you?'

'He was fifteen. I was nineteen.'

'I see. Do you understand that Rigby Hewitt was below the age of consent? And you were not? Do you understand, in fact, that what you were doing was against the law?'

What was the point in hesitating? 'Yes,' said Bazza.

'And did you understand that then?'

'I don't think we even thought about it.'

'No, I see. In a moment I'm going to ask you to describe for the recording exactly what is happening in that photograph. Before I do, please give me the name of the other person in this photograph.'

'That's Michael Saville.'

'Thank you, Barry. But that still leaves one mystery, doesn't it? Who was behind the camera, Barry? Who took the photograph?'

'That was Howard Diller.'

'Thank you. And was Howard Diller engaged in the same illegal activity as the rest of you?'

'Yes. Yes, he was.'

'Thank you, Barry. And now, please tell us exactly what is happening in this photograph. Start with where it was taken.'

'It was taken in Terence Carpenter's bedroom. His parents were away somewhere – don't ask me where, because at this distance in time I can't remember. In the photograph, Terence Carpenter is having sex with Rigby Hewitt while the rest of us hold Hewitt down.'

'Rigby Hewitt didn't want Terence Carpenter to have sex with him?'

'I expect he did. That's what he'd gone there for. He'd had sex with all of us in the past.'

Sally Barnes said, 'Clarify this for us, Barry. When you say he'd had sex with all of you, do you mean full penetrative anal intercourse? Or something else?'

'I mean what you said.'

'Full penetrative anal intercourse?'

'That. Yes.'

'And had he had it with all of you more than once? And had he been a willing participant?'

'Yes, and yes. Rigby was an absolute little tart. It takes young people like that sometimes – when they first find out what sex can be like, they're at it like rabbits and they can't get enough.' He looked at her out of the corner of his eye. 'I imagine it's much the same for straight people.'

'Then why are you holding him down in the photograph, Barry?'

'Oh, he was playing silly buggers. Pretending he hadn't known the rest of us would be there and didn't want us involved. It's just games people play.'

'Barry,' said Gareth. 'You have admitted the gang rape of a minor.'

Bazza shrugged.

'And now, Barry, we come to offences potentially even more serious than that. Two of the people with whom you carried out that rape are now dead. Murdered.'

Bazza's face turned the colour of chalk. 'Two? But... Who...'

'Michael Saville is dead, Barry. Killed in exactly the same way as Terence Carpenter.'

Cyril Bonser placed his hand on Bazza's arm. 'Constable, I request a few minutes with my client.'

153

Gareth looked at Sally and nodded. Sally said, 'We'll leave you. Let us know when you're ready to resume.'

***

When Gareth and Sally joined Blazeley and Susanna, Sally said, 'Do we know who Howard Diller is?'

'There's no one by that name in our jurisdiction. There are five Howard Dillers in the country and we have their local police forces looking them up.'

Blazeley said, 'We don't have enough on Humphries yet to charge him with the murders of Carpenter and Saville. I'm not sure we'll ever have enough, because I'm not convinced he did it. I don't see what his reasons would have been.'

Susanna said, 'I think you may be right. All right, breaking someone's nose shows he has a temper, but it wasn't temper that set up those two killings. It was careful planning.'

Blazeley said, 'It's your call, Susanna, but my instinct would be, when the interview is over, speak to CPS to authorise a charge of rape of a person under the age of consent. That's enough to hold him. Tomorrow we get him into court and ask for him to be remanded in custody. Then we'll have plenty of time to question him. Meantime, who knows what else we might turn up? As soon as he's charged we need to get SOCO into his flat.'

'Okay, boss,' said Susanna. Her phone rang and

she said, 'Hold on a moment while I answer this.' The phone conversation was a short one at the end of which she said, 'Thank you very much. I'm grateful. The findings you describe are so similar to two cases we are handling here that I'm sure my SIO, DCI Blazeley, will agree to us taking primacy. Yes, I'll tell him. If I set off now, I wouldn't be with you until so late it would be pointless. I'll get there as early in the morning as I can. Will you please get your pathologist to wait the post-mortem until I arrive? And, of course, secure the scene? Thank you. Till tomorrow.'

'Diller?' asked Blazeley.

Susanna nodded. 'That was Kettering police. They called on the Howard Diller who lives there and found him dead. Stripped naked, strangled, semen on his stomach. I said... Well, you heard what I said.'

'And you were right. Gareth, Sally, there's no need for Humphries or his lawyer to know about this yet. Wait till you get word that their parley is over; then get back down there, say something new has come up, charge him as we've just discussed, tell him he'll be taken to court tomorrow to be remanded and stick him in a cell. Susanna, you're going to have a very early start in the morning, so why don't you go home now? I'll brief the troops, organise SOCO and get HOLMES updated and I'll make sure you're kept up to date.'

'Thanks, boss. Might be an idea to update the

Superintendent, too.'

***

While this was going on, Cyril Bonser was talking to Bazza in the custody suite interview room. Bazza said, 'What did you mean by minimising the pain?'

'You're going to end up in court and you won't be able to plead not guilty. Not with what they have on tape now. Don't get any ideas about denying it or claiming it was made under duress – remember, they were filming you as well as recording what you said. But there were four witnesses to the original offence – the boy, and the three other men. We don't know what the boy is going to say when he gets into the witness box. Really, the police are supposed to brief us on everything they've said to him and he's said to them, but you'd better assume that won't happen. But two of those other witnesses are dead – so we know exactly what they are going to tell the court: two thirds of three eighths of sweet Fanny Adams. That leaves the third witness – Howard Diller. They know about him because you gave them his name. They'll find him, question him and charge him. If I'm able to talk to his lawyer before that happens, we can put together an approach that may get you a much reduced sentence. Maybe even suspended. Even if that doesn't happen, you may have spent long enough on remand by then to be released as soon as you are sentenced – and I'm

156

going to suggest that, when they take you into court tomorrow, we don't ask for bail. Four of you committed a criminal offence and now two of you are dead. You may be next on the killer's list, which means that jail may be the safest place for you. Apart from which, being in jail on remand is no one's idea of fun, but it's a lot better than being there after sentencing. Especially with the sort of crime you are accused of. Some of the most unpleasant people you've ever met are banged up, and you may be amazed by how righteous they can be about the crimes other people have committed. People like you.'

'They'll take me into court tomorrow?'

'They haven't said so yet, but you can count on it. Don't worry, that's not the trial – the trial won't happen for ages. But they need to remand you. You can be remanded on bail or in custody and for the time being – until they catch the killer – I'm recommending custody. I need to talk to Diller's lawyer and I can't do that till I know where Diller is. Right now, he's walking around, free as a bird, not even suspecting he needs a lawyer. So where do I find him?'

CHAPTER 18

There had been an underlying reason for Susanna's suggestion that Superintendent McAvoy should know what was going on. Yes, of course, as Head of Major Crime he should be told – but what she was hoping was that he'd leave work now, since it was very close to the time at which normal people who didn't have murders to solve went home, and she'd have the chance to see him that evening. Her hope was fulfilled when she received a text message suggesting she go straight to his place and he'd see her there.

One of the things she was learning was how hard it could be to switch off. Her head was buzzing with what had now become three deaths. What she really wanted to do was to spend an evening with the man she loved, talking about the things that mattered to them as a couple. That was easier said than done.

Chris said, 'I've got some halibut. It's one of my favourite fish. I thought I'd bake it with herbs and a touch of garlic and serve it with a salad and new potatoes. What do you think?'

'Well,' she said, 'I certainly don't want any potatoes someone's already used.'

'I'll take that as a yes. If we're still hungry afterwards, we can have cheese. Or, do you know, I think I have some ice cream cones wrapped in chocolate in the freezer.'

She wrapped her arms around him. 'I'm so lucky to have fallen for a guy who loves to cook.'

'Cooking for yourself is sort of thankless but a job that has to be done and it's better to do it well than badly. Cooking for someone else is an act of love. A chance to show how you feel. To nurture them.'

'Did you cook for Paula?'

'I certainly did. Paula had many gifts, but cooking was not among them. She saw food as fuel – something you filled up on but didn't notice. But she liked to be nurtured, too. And right now I get the feeling that you need a bit of nurturing.'

'Does it show? I was trying to keep it hidden.'

'Susanna, a murder case is difficult. Everyone feels that. When you investigate any crime, you're trying to do your best for people who've been damaged. But murder is more than that. For a start, you can never put it right – you can't bring the dead back to life. And it's so difficult to understand. Intellectually, we know all the motives: jealousy, lust, money, revenge – there are more, but not many. But what any normal human being finds difficult to understand is how any of those motives can drive someone to take someone else's life. And you, my love, are a normal human being.'

'And there was me thinking you saw me as Superwoman.'

'You are that, too. But I'm right, am I not? You've got all that going on inside you.'

In a subdued voice, Susanna said, 'Yes. I have. I'm sorry.'

'Don't be. If you didn't feel that way, you wouldn't be the person I've fallen in love with. All I can do is be with you, cook for you, and hear you.'

'Actually, Chris, I can think of another service you can provide for me. But it will mean going to bed quite soon after we finish eating, because I have to be up at the crack of dawn to get to Kettering in time for a busy day.'

He kissed her on the forehead. 'I'd better get on with this halibut.'

***

When Jamie Pearson got home after his shift that day, he still didn't know what he was going to do. Tell MCIT or not tell them? Jamie had no career ambitions in that direction. He loved what he did and he hadn't even taken sergeants' exams. He was content to remain a uniformed PC, serving the public in whatever ways he could to take away the guilt he still felt about turning away when Rita needed him. If he went to Rayyan Padgett or Susanna David, what would he tell them? It felt a bit thin as a story when he really thought about it, and he didn't want to end up feeling patronised. On the other hand, nor did he want to be remembered as the man who delayed the conclusion of a case by keeping to himself information he should have shared. He had done nothing about it that day, apart from telling Theresa McErlane what had been troubling him, and she had not in the end provided a firm opinion.

He valued Theresa's ideas. She was seven years younger than him, she had taken the sergeants' exams, and he knew that in her heart she longed for a move into Major Crimes Investigation. He wasn't sure he understood that – detectives had heavier workloads than any normal person could be expected to bear and their personal time could be interfered with just like that. Nevertheless, he knew it was what Theresa wanted and he hoped she would get her wish.

It would be an upheaval for him, though. Getting used to a new partner was always difficult at first. And then there was the question of what that new partner would be like. Jamie knew that his steady nature and years in the job meant that he tended to be assigned young partners straight out of training – that was what had happened with Theresa and, if he thought about it, it had also been true of her predecessor.

Well, mentoring a new PC was something that had real value. He should probably be proud that he was used in that way. In fact, he was proud. He turned to the most important matter now at hand. What was he going to eat tonight? Well, what was in the fridge? The answer to that was: not much. But in his vegetable bins he had potatoes and half a Savoy cabbage. And in a cupboard was a tin of corned beef. So that was the answer: corned beef

161

hash and cabbage with a healthy dollop of brown sauce. Was brown sauce in fact healthy? He didn't know. But he did know he enjoyed it.

***

Rita and Deborah, because they had to hand back the hired car and then take a train, got home later than either Susanna or Jamie. What they were going to eat was an issue for them, too, because Deborah had to work a double shift at the hospital the next day and needed a reasonable minimum of sleep tonight. They also wanted to do a little celebrating, and Rita and Deborah had their own way of celebrating – though one they shared with countless others. Including, though they could not know that, Susanna and Chris.

And so they settled on a fish supper which they picked up from the chippy at the end of the road washed down with a bottle of Prosecco that had been cooling in the fridge.

Later, when they had eaten, loaded the dishwasher, showered and romped in bed till they were both satisfied, Rita lay beside the sleeping Deborah and thought about the way her life had gone. It wasn't that she couldn't sleep; sleep would come when it was ready and until then she was happy just to let thoughts and scenes pass through her mind.

Twenty years had passed since that day, and that was still how she thought about it: That Day. A young girl's dreaming had taken her to the Rec.

She'd seen the way Jamie Pearson looked at her and she felt good about it. Jamie was exactly the sort of boy Rita would like to look at her in that way. What she wanted was for Jamie to do more than look – she wanted him to talk to her. Take her to one side. Let his interest be seen. And not just by her; if other girls saw that she could appeal to someone like Jamie, her stock would rise.

She hadn't wanted more than that. She hadn't been ready for more than that. And she certainly hadn't been ready for what happened instead. Those three louts, leaping on her, bearing her to the ground. They'd been like animals.

Terence Carpenter had been the worst. She'd never liked him. Most of the time that hadn't mattered because he wasn't there – he was away at some school which was no doubt where he'd acquired that sense of entitlement. That feeling that, if he wanted something, there was no reason he shouldn't have it. Including her.

The experience itself had been dreadful and she wasn't even going to think about it, had never thought about it, had blanked any recollection from her mind. But the aftermath was even worse.

She'd got home in tears, screaming, and they only had to look at her to know what she'd been through. She expected her mother to call the police and her father to rush out of the house and wreak vengeance on those who had outraged his daughter. Instead of which...

'It's your word against theirs,' said her father.

'Three against one. If the police will even take it to court, which they probably won't, how do you expect to be believed? They'll say you were willing. They'll drag your reputation through the mud. People will call you a slut.'

'But there were other people there,' she screamed. 'Witnesses!'

'Who?' her father wanted to know.

'Jamie,' she said. 'Jamie Pearson. He was there. And he wasn't the only one.'

'So what did he do, this Jamie Pearson, when they were...' His voice tailed off; he didn't want to finish the sentence, didn't want to put it into words.

And she couldn't really remember, because she'd been under the combined weight of three rampaging men, but she didn't think he'd been there at the end. When she'd run, knowing that she was bleeding, feeling as though she'd been ripped apart and brought as low as it was possible to go – had she seen him? She didn't think she had.

Her mother had gone out of the room as the conversation raged, but her father's will was stronger than Rita's and he wasn't going to wreak any vengeance or call any police. Then her mother came back and put her arms around Rita and said, 'I've run you a bath. Let's get you upstairs. It will look better in the morning.'

It will look better in the morning... What a stupid thing to have said. It hadn't looked better in the morning, or the morning after that, or any

164

morning. Rita had had to leave school because everyone knew what had happened and some had even watched it and she couldn't face them. For three months, she hadn't been out of the house. What she realised during that time was that what most concerned her parents was fear that she might be pregnant. The shame that would bring on the family would be even worse because no one would know who the father was.

It was that realisation of how far her own family had abandoned her that gave Rita the strength to begin her recovery. Deborah would later interpret for her that what she had been through in terms of something called transactional analysis. "What every child needs to feel when it looks at its family can be summed up as: I'm okay; you're okay. At the outset, when it's just born and until it can walk, feed itself and keep itself clean, the child feels very strongly that it's not okay – it depends absolutely on the adults who care for it – but as long as the family is okay, and as long as the family is working to make the child come to feel okay, that doesn't matter. It's normal development. But sometimes the child realises that its family is not okay. Then the child has to make the decision: will I take charge or not? You did. You said to your family, in effect, you're not okay, so I have to be okay." But Rita hadn't met Deborah yet. And when she did meet Deborah and when, quite a bit later, Deborah told her about I'm okay, you're okay, Deborah did not add that

165

therapists believed that the decision Rita had made without knowing she was making it – the decision that she was okay and the rest of the world was not – was what formed psychopaths.

Rita at school had been good at many subjects, but her favourite had always been art. And so she announced that she was going to go to art school. When her father began to explain to her what a silly idea that was, and that art school was not for people from families like Rita's, Rita let him speak a few sentences and then said, 'I'm sorry if you're not hearing clearly today. I'm going to art school.' Her father stared at her but said no more. When a few days later she put the forms in front of him and said she could get a grant, but only if he added his signature, he signed without a word. He and Rita's mother had begun to look at Rita in a different way. And perhaps they were motivated just a little by the thought she might find somewhere else to live.

Art school was everything Rita had hoped it would be. She turned out to be particularly good at drawing. Before her third year was up, she had sold a number of drawings and been offered a full-time job, which she was told she could do at the company's own premises or she could work from home. The art she would be producing would be commercial and not fine, but Rita didn't care about that. She was popular with the other girls and also with the boys, though more than one of them thought of her as "the ice maiden" when it became clear that she didn't reject their approaches so much as simply not notice them. There was a barrier between Rita and the male sex, born of Rita's knowledge of what the male sex was capable of.

Just before graduation, in a pub with some of her fellow students, Rita noticed a woman about ten years older than her looking at her in much the same way as Jamie had once done. It had never occurred to her that the approach she would accept instead of not noticing it might come from someone of her own sex. Nevertheless, she was aware of glancing in the woman's direction more often than she might have done. And the woman saw.

Rita went to the ladies' room. When she came out, the woman was by the door. She took Rita's hand in hers and let her to a car park at the back. It was late and it was dark. Rita had gone to the car park willingly and willingly she allowed herself to be turned round and pressed against the wall. The woman said, 'Kiss me, babe. I'm fireproof.' And Rita kissed her, without hesitation and without restraint.

The woman was Deborah, and Deborah had the advantage over Rita of having both a house of her own and a car. Without giving her fellow students a single thought, Rita got into the car and went to the house where she allowed herself to be undressed and was introduced to things that amazed her, but did not repel. When she woke at five the next morning, she found Deborah also awake and looking at her. 'Tell me about yourself,' Deborah said.

'Shouldn't you have found out about me before we did the things we did? I might be a complete nutter.'

Deborah said, 'You're not a nutter. Not a dangerous nutter – I've met a few, and I can tell. That's why I transferred from psychiatric nursing to looking after people who aren't going to survive. Now tell me about Rita.'

And Rita did, and one of the things she told Deborah was about the job that was waiting for her and that she could do it at home but she didn't have the right kind of home. Deborah said, 'Come with me' and led her to a room on the top floor. The roof was nothing but windows.

Rita said, 'I bet the light in here is fantastic.'

Deborah said, 'I inherited this place from my mother. She was an artist, too, and this was where she worked.' Rita looked at Deborah, unwilling to make the approach herself. Deborah said, 'It's fate. You must see that. Come and live with me. This room can be your studio.'

Rita said, 'What rent would you want?'

Deborah turned Rita as she had the previous evening and pressed against her. 'I'm inviting you to be my lover, not my lodger.'

They were so close to each other, Rita could feel Deborah's warm breath on her face. She put her arms round Deborah and hugged her. How did she feel about this? She felt fantastic – it was meant to be. Fate, as Deborah had said. The most natural thing in the world. Perhaps not for ever, but certainly for now. They kissed, and Deborah whispered, 'Come back to bed.'

Now here she was, seventeen years later, looking at the sleeping Deborah and feeling as besotted as she had those first few days in her company. The good fairies had been looking after her when they brought her and Deborah together. Sure, they'd argued and fought from time to time – that's what partners did – but Deborah had cared for her and looked after her in a way she could never have expected from a man. Rita still wasn't sure they'd be together for ever, but she was in no hurry to move on.

It had taken a while, but eventually Deborah had got out of her the story of her rape. 'It's all right to use that word,' Deborah had said. 'You don't have to keep referring to That Day, or What They Did to Me. They raped you. You can say it. The question is: what are we going to do about it?' And that, too, had taken a while. Rita had accepted that the three men had got away scot free and revenge was impossible. Deborah had had other ideas. And, bit by bit, Deborah had brought Rita to share those ideas.

When Rita thought back to the girl she had once been – the girl who had gone to the Rec because of the way a boy had looked at her – it seemed impossible that they had now killed three men and were planning the death of another (or, in Deborah's case, two more). And yet, she felt no guilt. They had had it coming.

Was it a coincidence that two of the men – Carpenter and Saville – who had attacked her had also done what they did to Rigby Hewitt? Probably not. People who would do something like that were people who would do something like that. One of the three they'd killed – Howard Diller – hadn't even been one of the three who had attacked Rita. But that didn't matter. Killing him was a way to throw the police off the scent. And let's face it, the guy may have been innocent of what had happened to Rita, but he was still guilty. He'd simply chosen a different victim. A victim who she and Deborah had now avenged.

And when she thought about it, it might even be possible that she and Deborah had done at least one of those men a favour. She remembered Michael Saville's response with something approaching tenderness. He'd known who she was – he remembered that whole horrible business and he was sorry. He'd said so. "Rita. I'm so, so sorry." That's what he'd said. And he'd said it just before Deborah eased his journey into the endless dark – and while Rita was making him feel better than he had any reason to expect about life and about himself. There had been no gentleness when he'd followed Carpenter and had his way with her. He could not have complained if they had subjected him to the same humiliation and the

170

same pain. And they had not.

Angels, you might call them. Avenging angels. And it was Deborah who had given her the power to be an avenging angel. She owed Deborah everything. But Ralph Townsend was going to be the last. Ralph Townsend had done to her what Terence Carpenter and Michael Saville had done, and he deserved to suffer the same fate. And that would be the end. Though it would be no surprise if Deborah added Bazza Humphreys to the list, now that Howard Diller had given them his name, just to confuse the police even more and throw them further off the scent. But not Jamie Pearson. She knew Deborah wanted to add Jamie, and she thought she knew why. Deborah believed that Rita had not entirely forgotten about Jamie, or given up hope that one day she and Jamie might even now bridge the gap that existed between them.

Was Deborah wrong?

That was Rita's business, and not Deborah's.

CHAPTER 19

Kettering was a three-hour drive from Batterton, and Susanna was on the road at five. That gave her time to stop at a service station for a bacon sandwich, coffee, a visit to the Ladies and to fill the fuel tank and still arrive before nine in the morning. She was shown straight into the office of DCI Merrill Perkins who offered her more coffee and introduced a DI and a detective sergeant. She said, 'I can't say I'm sorry you're taking this off our hands. If there's a serial killer wandering around, I'd rather someone else was looking for him. Nevertheless, you can count on us for any help you need.'

'Thank you, ma'am,' said Susanna. 'In fact, we think the serial killer may well be a her and not a him.'

'Good grief! Has there been a female serial killer before now?'

'I'm sure there must have been,' said Susanna, who in fact knew that there had been several.

'I suppose you're right. Beverley Allitt. Rosemary West. Myra Hindley.'

And Joanna Dennehy, thought Susanna. And Mary Elizabeth Wilson. And... Well, why go on about it? Women were killers, just like men were.

DCI Perkins said, 'Sergeant Tremain here will show you the crime scene. He'll also take you to the post-mortem, which is scheduled for two this afternoon. That means you won't be getting away from Kettering until quite late and you have a long drive ahead of you, so I won't ask you to come back and tell me how the post-mortem goes – but if you can get back here at about twelve, DI Damski will be delighted to buy you lunch.' And she stood, and Susanna knew the meeting was over.

***

There was still crime scene tape across the gateway to Howard Diller's garden and a uniformed policeman was on watch. He logged the arrival of DS Tremain, who he clearly knew, and Susanna, who he did not and who he asked for her warrant card. 'You have well-trained people,' said Susanna.

Tremain's response could have been a grunt but Susanna couldn't really be sure because he was struggling his way into a scenes of crime suit that wasn't really big enough for his more than ample size. She had donned hers and her protective overshoes some time before Tremain was fully suited up. The house was still being examined and they trod carefully on the plates SOCO had put down. When they reached the kitchen, Tremain said, 'This is where he died.' He turned to the crime scene manager. 'Wendy, this is DI David. Would you mind talking her through the scene?'

The CSM went to the table. 'The body was on here. He was naked, he had been masturbated and he had been strangled using a cable tie. The clothes he'd been wearing were on the floor beside him. They've been bagged up; there was no sign of any blood or bodily fluids on them, but we'll be asking for a DNA examination – that is, if your force will bear the cost.'

Susanna nodded. 'Go ahead.' Budgets everywhere were a problem and it was not reasonable to expect another force to bear the cost of expensive DNA examinations. She said, 'It's unusual to find the clothes. Usually, the killer takes them away with her.'

It was always difficult to tell when people had all that protective gear on, but Susanna was pretty sure the CSM's eyebrows had risen just a little when she heard the word, "her." What she said, though, was more interesting. 'I think you'll find we're dealing with more than one person here.'

'You think the killer had someone with her?'

'I'm sure of it. It will all be in our report, but there's no shortage of evidence: apart from the victim, there were two people here.'

'Thank you – that's very interesting. Anything else I should know?'

'Probably a great deal, but we don't know it ourselves yet. As I said, it will all be in our report and I'll get that to you as fast as I can.'

'Thank you. I'd better get out of your way and let you get on.'

Tremain walked her to the front door. He said, 'Door-to-door hasn't turned up very much as yet, and as you can see there's quite a lot of space between this house and the next one, but a lady in a house down the road saw a car sitting in the drive when she drove past. Unfortunately, she didn't see it arrive and she didn't see it leave and so she couldn't say how many people were in it. Nor can she say what kind of car it was, or even what colour. She said she thought it was probably black but it might have been red and it could possibly even have been blue, so pick the bones out of that. And, of course, we can't even be certain that the car brought the killers here. It does seem quite likely, though, because it seems that the occupier – Howard Diller – didn't have many visitors.'

Susanna said, 'It's a very nice house. And that kitchen must have cost a small fortune. What do we know about him so far?'

Tremain opened up his tablet. 'He lived alone. He worked as a consultant at the hospital here. We've got someone over there, seeing what they can dig up – if we find anything, we'll let you know. His phone has a very short list of contacts and they all seem to be work colleagues. He called someone a few days ago and the someone called him back.'

'Anyone interesting?'

'We haven't checked it. We thought you'd like to do that. Give me your phone number or your email and I'll send you the number.'

When they'd done that, and Susanna had forwarded the number to Marion Trimble and Bill

175

Blazeley, Tremain said, 'Apart from that, there isn't much to tell you. He seems to have lived quietly. The neighbours say he spent a lot of time working in his garden. The contents of his freezer and fridges suggest he was an enthusiastic cook – but you'd expect that, given the state of his kitchen. There were about thirty bottles in his wine rack and none of them cost less than fifteen pounds – some are a lot more. If you're done here, I'll get you back to the station. DI Damski can probably fill you in on any information from the hospital.'

***

On the way, Susanna took a call from DCI Blazeley. 'That phone number you sent us. It's registered to Michael Saville.'

'Well, that is interesting. So Saville called Diller, and Diller called Saville back, and now both of them are dead. I wonder what those calls were about. Did we ever find Saville's phone?'

'No, we didn't. I've asked SOCO to take another look, but you know it isn't there. If it had been, they'd have found it.'

'Well, at least it shows a clear link between the two men.'

'Yes, it does. If we knew what that link was, we'd probably be on our way to pick up the killer.'

'Actually,' said Susanna, 'it seems that should probably be killers.'

'Say that again,' said Blazeley.

'Diller had two visitors when he died. SOCO

didn't find evidence of more than one for either Carpenter or Saville – but in both those cases, the killer or killers had lots of time to clean up the scene. In Carpenter's case, they'd actually gone as far as vacuuming the house and taking the contents of the vacuum cleaner with them. And Saville – well, let's not forget the place he died. It could have been used as a pigsty without any modification and to be quite frank a pigsty is what it looked like. Kettering is a long way from either of those places and I think the killers must have been in more of a hurry to get away this time. Apart from anything else, they left the clothes the victim had been wearing and they haven't done that before. It seems very likely they came in a car, but we don't have a license plate and we don't know the make or model. Okay, I'm at the station now – I'll get back to you as soon as I know more.'

DI Damski welcomed Susanna, but seemed harassed. 'You know how it is because I'm sure it's the same for you – too many cases and not enough officers. Anyway, your dead hospital consultant. According to NHS HR, his work record was exemplary. We'd expect them to say that. I sent two very experienced guys there and they tried to speak to his closest friends but that wasn't possible. They weren't blocked – it seems Diller didn't have any friends where he worked. One interesting comment was that he wasn't cold, but he was distant. A male nurse who had worked with him quite a lot said that he thought Diller might quite possibly be gay, but he hadn't tried it on with the nurse or, as far as the nurse knew, anyone else. Kettering has the same gay scene as anywhere else in the country; would you like us to put out feelers and see if he was known in any of the clubs?'

'If you could,' said Susanna, 'that would be great.'

'Okay. What else is there? Family. We haven't turned any up yet; I assume someone gave birth to him, but there are no links on his phone, no entries in his phone book, no emails on his laptop that could have come from family members and no personal letters in his house. Either everyone is dead, or he's cut himself off completely. Or the other way round, of course – they may have cut themselves off from him. We are checking all the local firms of solicitors to see if he left a will with any of them – there isn't one in his house and people with an estate worth handing on usually want to make arrangements about what will happen to it. Susanna, the DCI promised me as a lunch companion and I'm happy to do that, but would you mind if I invited one of our sergeants to join us? He's been babysitting the victim of another offence as an FLO though he is far too senior for that – there were special circumstances – and I'm keen to hear what he has to say. It's time he was off duty and getting some kip.'

'That sounds fine to me,' said Susanna.

'Great. And after that, Sergeant Tremain will

178

take you to the post-mortem.'

***

Theresa McErlane had been touched by what Jamie Pearson had told her. Or not, in fact, by what he had told her but by what he had revealed about himself in the telling. Not touched enough to suggest they might spend some time together outside work; she was still resistant to dating someone she worked with. Still, Jamie had shown himself to be a decent sort of guy who didn't think he was superior to women simply by virtue of owning a pair of testicles. That was something.

She'd grown tired of the attitude of many of the men she worked with. She was ready to accept that things were improving, but they still had a long way to go and for too many men in the police force "male chauvinist pig" was unfair to the hog population. And Jamie didn't just behave nicely – he treated her as though he cared what she thought. He listened to what she said.

So, no, she didn't tell herself that she and Jamie might have a future outside this police car. She didn't even tell herself they had one inside it, because Theresa intended to get herself promoted and transferred into MCIT as soon as possible, and it was obvious that Jamie planned to stay exactly where he was until the day he retired.

But there was a thought. Because Theresa didn't just want a career in the police. She wanted what she'd grown up as part of – a happy family.

179

She wanted children. Children needed parental time if they were to grow up happy and balanced, as she had. And once she was in MCIT, her time would be much less her own. So was it a good idea for one of the parents to have a job that was a bit more regular than the life of a detective?

She wasn't going to go on thinking like that, because it couldn't lead anywhere. Still. It did no harm to let the thoughts pass through her mind from time to time. And if you were going to do something like that, Jamie was certainly the kind of man do it with.

He was nice looking, too. Her girlfriends wouldn't turn up their noses if they saw them together. There might even be a touch of envy.

***

It is always interesting to see how people do the job you do but do it somewhere else, but Susanna learned nothing new at lunch. The post-mortem began at two, as planned, and didn't end until just after six, so she already knew she was going to be late getting home to Batterton. She sent Chris McAvoy a text message saying so and that she would go straight home and straight to bed. She'd have to go there in any case, because she needed something different to wear when she went to work next morning. To make sure she was even later, after the post-mortem Tremain told her he'd been asked to take her back to the station.

When they reached there, the DI had already

left but the crime scene manager from the Howard Diller murder was waiting for her. 'We found the victim's will. It names a solicitor and the solicitor confirms that he has the original. We've bagged it up, and you can take it away, but we made this copy.'

Susanna read what she had been handed. It was very simple – Diller had left everything he had to his sister, and her address was given. Susanna said, 'She lives in Batterton. I wonder... Is that simple coincidence, or is that where Diller originally came from? Well, it's helpful because it means we can question her without any bother.' And she rang the Batterton police station to get three things done. To get the existence and details of Diller's will onto HOLMES. To get a new action onto the system, the action being to visit Howard Diller's sister, tell her he was dead and find out what they could. And to get that visit under way without delay.

'Two other things,' said the CSM. 'The DI left word to say that the three best-known gay clubs in town have been questioned, and Howard Diller was not known in any of them.'

'Thank you,' said Susanna. 'But perhaps his sister will be able to tell us more. The second thing?'

'Fingerprints in Diller's kitchen. One person who left them has their prints on file.'

'My God! That could be the breakthrough. Who do they belong to?'

'Well, let's not get too excited. We don't know that they are connected with the murder. They might have been left months ago. Although that does seem unlikely; there were very few different lots of prints. Diller kept his kitchen spotless.'

'Don't keep me in suspense!'

'Right. Well, bearing in mind the caveat I just mentioned, the prints belong to a woman called Sadie McIntosh. She was a nurse and she was jailed for manslaughter twenty years ago. A patient she was looking after died. That's all I can tell you – you have the same access to the records as we do.'

CHAPTER 20

Nicola and Rayyan were given the task of calling on Howard Diller's sister, who according to Diller's will was now called Cynthia Barber. Knocking on someone's door at approaching seven in the evening can have mixed results: you're more likely to find the person you want to speak to at home, but you may well be interfering with their dinner time. Cynthia brushed aside proffered apologies: 'Don't worry about it. My husband is out of town, we don't have any children and I've already eaten. When he's away, that's my opportunity to eat the kind of things I like instead of things that suit us both. And I like stir-fried vegetables. But why do the police want to speak to me? I know it isn't my husband, because I just put the phone down on him. But come in.'

She showed them into a sitting room that was comfortable without being expensive. Thinking about what they'd already heard from Kettering, it occurred to Nicola that Cynthia Barber would soon be able to afford something far more luxurious than she had at the moment. Rayyan, as the senior officer, started the conversation. 'Mrs Barber, are you the sister of Howard Diller?'

The change in Cynthia's bearing was immediate. 'Howard? My God. What's happened?'

'Is he your brother? Yes?'

'Yes. YES! What's happened to him?'

Rayyan said, 'I'm afraid Mr Diller is dead. And we are treating the death as suspicious.'

Suspicious, thought Nicola. You can say that again. Not many people with a cable tie around the throat turn out to have died of natural causes.

Cynthia Barber had slumped into a chair. The two detectives took the opportunity to sit down opposite her. She said, 'How did you find me?'

'Your name and address are in his will, Mrs Barber,' said Rayyan. 'You are the only beneficiary.'

Cynthia was simply staring past Rayyan's shoulder. Nicola had seen this before – shock would make the poor woman incapable of much logical thought for a little while, but this was a murder case and they needed to get as much information as they could. She said, 'Mrs Barber... Cynthia... We do realise what a shock this must have been and how you must be feeling at this moment, but the first hours of a murder investigation are vital if we are to find the person responsible. I'm sorry to have to press you at a time like this, but what can you tell us about your brother's life?'

'Nothing. I can tell you nothing... I'm sorry, you're going to have to wait a moment.' She picked up her phone and pressed a quick dial button. 'Darling? Darling, the police are here. Howard is dead. Murdered. I'm sorry, I know it's inconvenient, I know it may be damned awkward, but I need you to come home, please. I know what I'm asking but I can't be on my own tonight and there's no way I'm going to Mum and Dad's.' As she listened to her husband, the tension seemed to seep away. 'Thank you, darling. Thank you so much. I don't suppose you've eaten yet – I'll get something out of the freezer for you.' She put the phone down. 'He'll be here in about two hours. Now – what did you want to know?'

'Your brother, Cynthia,' said Nicola. 'What can you tell us about his life?'

'Nothing,' she said again. 'Well… Obviously, that's not true. But I can't tell you why he may be… Why someone would kill him, because I haven't seen him or heard from him for years. You just heard me talking to my husband; we were married fifteen years ago and he has never met Howard.'

'He knew who he was, though,' said Rayyan. 'That was clear from the way you spoke.'

'Oh, yes,' said Cynthia. 'He knows who Howard was, all right.'

***

No shrinking violet ever succeeds in mainstream journalism. Bernie Spence was not going to be content to spend her whole working life with a regional newspaper. She wanted the bright lights – London, the nationals, national television. She knew what it took to get there, and Bernie was ready to forego sleep and to work like a mad thing until she had the story she wanted. Right now, the stories she wanted concerned Terence Carpenter and Michael Saville. And, because he was less prominent, Michael Saville above all.

The first thing she did was talk to the man who rented the two fields where Saville had died. The police press release had not identified the exact location, but a trip to Oswestry and questions in pubs and coffee shops (of which Oswestry turned out to have a large number) soon pinpointed the ex-canal worker's ruined cottage. Parking in the middle of the field caught the farmer's attention and he told her where to find his tenant. 'He's a hippie,' he said. 'Harmless – we have a stack of them in the hills around here. They started arriving in the 60s and never left. I don't know how they all live, but they seem to survive.'

The "hippie" was happy to talk to Bernie in return for two wraps she brought with her. 'Thanks,' he said. 'I usually rely on a neighbour, but he got busted. Anyway, free is better. What do you want to know?'

When that conversation was over, she sought out Carol Watts, Michael Saville's partner. Then she went back to Batterton and looked for Saville's parents and then for his brother, Donald. When it became clear that she would get nothing out of the parents and that Donald would not go against their wishes, she let it be known that she was keen to talk to anyone who had known Michael before he left Batterton.

When all of that was done, she sat down and hammered out a piece for the next morning's Post. Her editor, when he saw it, said, 'Well done, Bernie,' and approved it without amendment. Then he passed her a press release from Kettering police station about Howard Diller.

'Does this matter to us?' said Bernie. 'Kettering's bloody miles away.'

'Yes, it is,' said the editor. 'But Diller was from here. His parents still live here, and so does his sister. If you get a move on, you'll have a nice follow-up to the Saville piece.'

However much she tried, Bernie had not yet mastered the art of hiding her surprise, and she didn't now. 'You think they're connected?'

'A little bird tells me that DI Susanna David drove all the way to Kettering, spent time closeted with detectives there, and attended Diller's post-mortem. So, yes – I wouldn't be the slightest bit surprised if they're connected.'

When Bernie left the editor's office, she was aware of just how tired she was and that she had a choice: to follow this up now, or to get the sleep she desperately needed. A journalist on the make with the amount of ambition that drove Bernie knows she'll always be able to sleep tomorrow. She already knew she needed to find Rita. Now she set about establishing where to find Diller's parents.

***

187

Susanna knew that she had little chance of reaching Batterton before ten if she drove without stopping, and she needed something to eat. She therefore stopped on the way. The best she could find to eat was a gammon steak with fried eggs and chips, and so that and a mug of tea were what she had. She promised herself that she would eat better tomorrow. That would be easier if she made it to Chris's place and let him feed her.

She got home at nearly eleven, showered and went to bed, setting her alarm so that she'd be likely to reach the station next morning at the very least no later than Bill Blazeley and ideally before him. After another shower and breakfast of toast, marmalade and tea, she found herself parking at exactly the same time as the DCI. That, she told herself, was good enough.

Blazeley smiled to see her. 'No one would have blamed you if you'd slept in this morning. You must have had a desperately late night. Seen this?' And he handed her a copy of that morning's newspaper. Susanna took one look at the front page and said, 'I need to read this over a cup of tea.'

'Let's go upstairs and talk about it.'

Deaths of Two Local Men
Bernadette Spence

A second man with his roots in Batterton has died in circumstances police say are suspicious. On Saturday, we reported the death of local lawyer Terence Carpenter, who the police have now confirmed was murdered. Yesterday, the body of Michael Saville, 48, was found in a disused lock-keeper's cottage on the Montgomery Canal on the border between England and Wales. He, too, was murdered and sources close to the police say that he and Carpenter met their death in ways too like each other to be coincidental.

Saville had lived for many years close to the place where he was found dead, but he was born and brought up in Batterton. He told his partner, Carol, that he was an orphan, but in fact he is survived by his parents and his brother Donald, 39, who still live here. When approached, they refused to speak about Michael. Family friends told this reporter that a rift had occurred in the family about twenty years ago. Michael left Batterton for University that same year and never returned. His parents have disowned him and refused to acknowledge that they ever had a son of that name. Friends were unwilling to reveal the details of the rift, and would go no further than to say that it was caused by Michael Saville's treatment of a young girl which was described as "vile" and "completely beyond the pale."

Police are at a loss to know what connection between the two men caused them to be murdered in the same way, but sources say that the connection is proved beyond doubt.

'Sources and family friends,' said Blazeley. 'Often used by journalists to hide the fact that they made something up. But also often used when someone has given them information and doesn't want to be identified. We don't know which it is this time – but Bernie Spence has a name for hard work and attention to detail.'

'She talks about treatment of a young girl,' said Susanna. 'We are investigating treatment of a young man. Have they said girl because they don't remember? To hide the facts? Or are we barking up the wrong tree?'

'Only one way to find out, Susanna. You'll have to talk to her.'

Susanna pursed her lips. 'She gave me the chance to do that and I turned it down.'

'She won't mind. She's waiting to hear from you, now that that report is out. Get on to the Post and invite her for a chat.'

***

But Bernie Spence was not waiting quietly for Susanna's arrival. When Susanna called, the

Post's editor said she was out and he didn't know when she'd be back. He gave Susanna Bernie's mobile phone number, but it went straight to voicemail. Bernie wasn't answering a call from the police because she was in full cry after her current prey – Rita Taylor. The "family friends" she'd referred to were neighbours of the Saville family who remembered very clearly what Michael Saville and two other men had done to a defenceless girl and also remembered the girl's name.

And so, when the morning briefing went ahead, Susanna was there. They went through the outstanding matters as fast as possible, with Marion Trimble reading them out from HOLMES and the relevant detectives providing the answers. Credenza Carpenter had been found living in Berwick-upon-Tweed under the name of Pat Carpenter. 'Not married, then,' said Susanna. 'And she's gone as far from Batterton as she could get while staying in England.'

'If you can call Berwick in England,' said Blazeley. 'It's as Scottish as Dundee – though Dundee is a rather nice place and Berwick is a dump. But that's not what you're thinking about, is it? You're wondering whether she was the girl in this morning's newspaper. The one to whom Michael Saville did something so vile and so completely beyond the pale that his parents refuse to acknowledge his existence. Which might have caused her to stay single and to get as far as she

191

could from the place where it happened.'

'It crossed my mind,' admitted Susanna. 'But Credenza would not have been a girl when Michael Saville was university entrance age.'

Blazeley said, 'It's a funny word, girl. My wife goes on holiday every year with three women she was at school with. They refer to each other as "the girls." None of them is less than fifty.'

'Yes,' said Susanna, 'we'd better bear it in mind. What else is there, Marion?'

A detective sergeant raised his hand. 'DC Parker and I went house to house in Barracuda Street. Nobody had CCTV pointing in the right direction, and nobody admitted seeing Terence Carpenter on the evening in question. A complete dead end, I'm afraid. Sorry.'

'Don't be,' said Blazeley. 'I've said it before; I may very well have to say it again – every time one lead is closed off, we get that much closer to the end. Marion, what else have you got?'

'DNA results from the Michael Saville killing are in. The semen on Saville's stomach was his own; there was additional DNA on his penis and it matched what was found on Carpenter's. Whoever masturbated Carpenter masturbated Saville.'

'Well,' said Blazeley, 'there wasn't really any doubt, but if there had been it would now be removed. The same person killed Carpenter and Saville. And, almost certainly, Howard Diller – we'll know for sure when we get his DNA results, but I'll be amazed if it's otherwise. And, that being the case, let's remember that we are looking for two killers and not one. Yes, Marvin,' he said to a DC who had raised his hand.

'Sir,' said Marvin. 'If there are two killers working together, and if the DNA evidence shows that one masturbates the victim, should we be assuming that the other kills the victim at the moment of climax?'

'It's a very good working hypothesis,' said Blazeley. 'We should certainly keep it in mind as a theory that stands up, at least for now.' He looked towards Marion, who shook her head. 'Nothing else right now, sir.'

'We have to add Sadie McIntosh to the mix,' said Blazeley. 'Susanna, I know how late it was when you got home last night, and I know how early you must have been up this morning, but what have you been able to find out about Sadie?'

'It wasn't hard to dig up,' said Susanna. 'The newspapers made a huge story out of it. She grew up in Hartlepool.'

'That's enough to make anyone a murderer,' murmured a DC.

'She was a registered nurse. She was working for an agency, looking after people who couldn't look after themselves. Old people, for the most part. Widowed old people, very often. Sometimes – not always, but sometimes – one of those old people was so grateful for the care Sadie lavished on them that they wrote her into their will. And, of course, she collected when they died – but dying is what old people do. The deaths were expected. In each case, a doctor signed a death certificate either naming a specific illness that had carried the patient away or giving it as natural causes. Those certificates went to the coroner, of course, as is usual, and the coroner decided there was nothing suspicious about the deaths. But in one case, the local police disagreed. The post-mortem showed an unduly high level of morphine. When she was questioned, Sadie McIntosh said she had given the patient more morphine than had been prescribed. She said the woman had been in great pain and she described what she had done as a mercy killing. If she hadn't received fifty thousand pounds in the patient's will, the jury might have agreed. But she had. She was found not guilty of murder but guilty of manslaughter and she served thirty months of a five year sentence. She's been out for quite some time, but what happened to her no-one seems to know. Of course, with a conviction like that, she wouldn't be allowed to nurse again. But there has been no sign since the day of her release of anyone called Sadie McIntosh of anything like the right age.'

'Okay,' said Blazeley. 'Marion, I want an action assigned to someone: track down Sadie McIntosh. Where is she? What name is she going under? Where does she live? What is she doing?'

'And while we are at it,' said Susanna, 'find out where she did her time and who else was in there with her.'

'What's your thinking, Susanna?'

'People are sent to jail for all kinds of things. Did Sadie McIntosh meet someone who could help her disappear and come back as someone else?'

'Good thinking. Anything else, anyone? No?' Blazeley was about to bring the meeting to an end when a uniformed sergeant came into the incident room with a package.' What's this?' asked Blazeley.

'It arrived in the post, sir. It's addressed to the officer in charge of the murders of Carpenter and Saville.'

'Is it? Susanna, get this opened in a controlled environment. We may find prints on the envelope and whatever is inside it. Everyone else – you know what you have to do. Go and do it. We'll meet here again this evening to review progress.'

CHAPTER 21

The day before, Jamie Pearson had begun a week of night duty. He had got home this morning shortly after eight, drunk a mug of tea into which he had dunked two digestive biscuits, showered and gone to bed. At about one, he was thinking about getting up and making himself some breakfast when he heard someone knocking at his door. He pulled on a pair of underpants and a dressing gown and answered the door to find on his doorstep a well-dressed, well-groomed woman a few years younger than him. She was holding a newspaper. 'Jamie Pearson?' she asked. 'Constable Pearson?'

He nodded. 'That's me.'

'May I come in? My name is Bernadette Spence. But friends call me Bernie.'

Bernadette thought of what she did when she first approached someone as "putting the charm on people." She had no idea how "the charm" worked, but it rarely failed her. Jamie stood back, let her come in, closed the door behind her and led the way to his kitchen. 'I was just thinking about something to eat. Would you like a cup of tea?'

'Love one, Jamie. And if you want to eat, don't let me stop you.'

Jamie's face expressed embarrassment. 'I've just realised I forgot to get anything in. I'm going to have to go to the shops before I can make my breakfast.'

'Well, that's easily dealt with. A place not far from here does all day breakfasts. Let's go there – the Post will pay.'

'The Post? Why should the Post pay for my breakfast?'

'That's who I work for, Jamie. And I want to ask you some questions about a story I'm investigating.'

'Oh, now wait a moment – I can't talk to a reporter. If you have questions, you need to go to the Press Office.'

'The questions are about Rita Taylor, Jamie. Specifically, about something that happened to her twenty years ago. Something not very nice at all. I've been talking to people. More than one of them said you were there.'

'I'm sorry. Talking to you would break every rule we have. I'd like you to leave.'

'Jamie, you look as though someone five times your size has just hit you in the solar plexus.'

'Please go.'

'Things don't get better if you ignore them, Jamie. People say time is a great healer, but that's nonsense. Time heals nothing. What does the healing is the work you do. And here's your chance. Unburden yourself. Get it off your chest. You know you want to.'

And she was right – he did want to. Someone had told him once that this was why they had training – so that they would make the right decision when the pressure was so great they were incapable of thinking. 'I won't tell you again. You're trespassing.'

'Don't be silly, Jamie. You invited me in. You even offered me a cup of tea. That's not trespassing.'

'You want to argue it out in front of magistrates?'

She sighed and stood up. 'Okay, Jamie. But here's my card. If you think better of it, call me. And I'm going to talk to Rita, just as soon as I find out where she is. And I will find out, Jamie. That's what I do. And whatever she tells me, I will print. You were there. If you don't want the public to hear your side of the story before they hear hers, there's nothing I can do about it. But I'm not sure you're making the right decision. I'll leave this paper here for you to read.'

He walked her to the front door, made sure she was on the other side of it, and closed it. Then he walked back into the kitchen, made a mug of tea, and picked up the paper.

A few minutes later, Jamie felt drained. All the things he'd tried for twenty years not to think about had come flooding back. The journalist had been right – he needed to get it off his chest. But not with her. He'd already talked about it once in the last few days, to Theresa, and he needed to talk about it again. He picked up the phone, rang the police station, and asked to speak to DI Susanna David. 'Sure,' she said. 'If it has to do with today's story in the Post, of course I have time to talk to you. When can you get here?'

Jamie realised that his need for breakfast was intense. Apart from the two digestive biscuits, he hadn't eaten anything since he'd wolfed down a cold meat pie in the car at ten the previous evening. He didn't want to face a DI on an empty stomach, and the journalist's suggestion of an all-day breakfast appealed enormously, as long as she wasn't watching him eat it. He said, 'About an hour from now?'

'I'll be waiting.'

That would work out very well. When he'd finished talking to her, he'd remember to do his food shopping. Stock up for the week ahead.

***

Blazeley, Susanna, Rayyan and Nicola listened to Howard Diller's taped confession. 'Well,' said Blazeley. 'Wasn't that interesting? As much for what it didn't tell us as for what it did. For example, it didn't tell us who the other person was who raped Rigby Hewitt. I don't doubt that omission was deliberate. Fortunately, we know it was Barry Humphries. Something more interesting the tape didn't tell us was who Diller was talking to. That's assuming it was Diller. So: why do we think that tape was sent to us? Anyone?'

Susanna said, 'I think, until we find out differently, we should assume that it really was

Diller. That's just based on the amount he knew. Would anyone who hadn't been there have known everything he said? It sounded very like a confession and the impression I got was that Diller thought he was talking to the police. I think we have to assume that whoever it was, it was one of the killers. Because only one person other than Diller spoke. But why – that's another question. I can understand that they might have wanted Diller to confess before they killed him. But why send it to us? Murder is murder; they surely can't think we'd say, oh well, in this case it was justified so we'll leave them.'

'No,' said Blazeley. 'They had some other reason for sending that tape to us. Did you get any prints off it?'

'Not off the tape, it had been wiped clean. There were a number of prints on the package, and you'd expect that. I imagine more than one postman has handled it. But there were two partials that match a print found in Diller's kitchen. They haven't left prints anywhere else. As you said, boss, they were in more of a rush in Kettering. Perhaps just because they were so far from home; perhaps for other reasons.'

Rayyan said, 'It does suggest, though, that they probably live here or hereabouts. They were rushed in Kettering; here, they took their time.'

'It does suggest that,' said Blazeley. 'But back to the reason. They turned the recording off at exactly the moment when Diller was about to name the other person. What that suggests to me is that they plan to bump off Barry Humphries and they don't know that we already have his name. And that just could give us an edge. But only if we let Humphries go home and stake him out like a sacrificial goat. I'm not tempted to do that, in case anything goes wrong and causes my career terminal damage.'

Susanna's phone buzzed. She listened to it and then said, 'Jamie Pearson.'

'Uniformed PC,' said Blazeley. 'Excellent man, but no ambition.'

'We need people like that,' said Susanna. 'We'd be in a mess if everyone wanted to be chief constable. But Jamie wants to talk to me about the story in today's Post. And he's downstairs.'

'Get him up here,' said Blazeley. 'Let's all hear what he has to say.'

When he realised he was going to be unburdening himself to four people, and one of them a chief inspector, Jamie wondered for a moment whether he was doing the sensible thing. The reality was that he'd started, and now he had to finish, so he decided to just tell the whole story. It was Susanna he'd come to see, so he'd speak to her.

'Ma'am, I had a visit from a woman called Bernadette Spence.'

'The journalist?'

'Her, ma'am. She wanted me to talk about Rita Taylor. I told her that it would be against our rules and that if she wanted information she had to go to the Press Office. She didn't like it, but she left.'

'You did the right thing, Jamie.'

'Yes, ma'am. But it's been in my mind for a few days that I needed to talk to you about Rita.'

'Rita Taylor. I don't think I…'

'Ma'am, twenty years ago, when she would have been fifteen or sixteen, Rita Taylor was raped by three men. One of them was Terence Carpenter. In fact, he was the ringleader. Another was Michael Saville.' He paused, aware that all four officers facing him had exchanged looks.

'I can see why you need to talk about it,' said Susanna. 'The third man – was his name Howard Diller?'

'Howard Diller? No, ma'am. The third man was Ralph Townsend.'

'I see. Jamie, how do you come to know about this?'

He didn't want to, but Jamie could not prevent himself from lowering his head. With an effort, he brought himself back up to look Susanna in the eye. 'Ma'am, I was there.'

Silence followed that statement. Then Blazeley said, 'Tell us exactly what happened. Don't miss anything out. Take your time, but tell the whole story, however insignificant bits of it may seem.'

'Yes, sir. It was here in Batterton, on the recreation ground close to where I lived as a boy. I'd gone there in the hope of seeing Rita.'

Blazeley nodded. 'You were sweet on her.'

'Yes, sir. I was a bit shy. I'd wanted to talk to her and I hoped, if she was there, I'd get up the courage to do it.' He looked around the four faces. There was no mockery, no ridicule and he wished he'd felt able to face all this a long time ago. 'But when she came, and before I could speak to her, those three attacked her. They were older than me and bigger than me. I know that's no excuse, but…'

'Yes it is,' said Blazeley. 'It wouldn't be now, because now you're a policeman and you'd be expected to step in whatever the odds. But twenty years ago… How old were you twenty years ago, Jamie?'

'I was sixteen, sir.'

'Sixteen. Have you been beating yourself up over this ever since? Because if you have, you need to stop.'

Susanna said, 'Did this have anything to do with you joining the police, Jamie?'

'It did, ma'am. I felt…' He tailed away, unsure how to continue.

Blazeley said, 'You felt guilty and you thought you wanted to do a better job of protecting people in the future.'

Jamie nodded. 'I know it must sound ridiculous but…'

'It doesn't sound any such thing. If there are better reasons for becoming a cop, I don't know what they are.'

'Sometimes, sir, I've wondered if I did the right

thing. When you see the things that happen. It was one of us that murdered Sarah Everard. It was one of us that kicked Dalian Atkinson to death.'

'There'll always be the bad apples, Jamie. But what the public relies on is that, for every Wayne Couzens and every Benjamin Monk, there are ten Jamie Pearsons. And I think, by and large, that's what they get.'

Susanna said, 'I just want to get two things clear, Jamie. And then we'll let you go, and I hope you'll be going in the knowledge that coming to see us was the best thing you could have done. But it was twenty years ago, and memory can be a slippery thing. The three men who raped Rita Taylor. You're quite sure one of them wasn't Howard Diller?'

'Quite sure, ma'am.'

'All right. If you're sure, you're sure. And the second thing: Do you know where Rita is now?'

'I'm afraid not, ma'am. No-one saw her for ages. She didn't come out of her house at all. And then, suddenly, she was gone. I heard she went to art school. I don't know if that's true, though.'

'Where did she live, Jamie? Before she left for art school?'

'Canberra Drive, ma'am. Number twenty-six.'

Susanna smiled. 'You have a good memory.'

'I'm not likely to forget anything to do with Rita, ma'am.'

When Jamie had left, Blazeley said, 'So. We now have competing reasons for the murder of

Terence Carpenter and Michael Saville. We thought they were killed in revenge for what happened to Rigby Hewitt. But it seems the revenge could also be for what happened to Rita Taylor.'

Rayyan said, 'But, sir, doesn't the murder of Howard Diller bring us back to Rigby Hewitt?'

'It might look that way,' said Blazeley. 'But maybe that's what we are meant to think. What I'm struggling with is: we know that at least one of the killers is female. It isn't impossible they both are. Why would a woman seek revenge for the gay rape of a man? Isn't it more likely that a woman would be involved in revenge for the rape of a woman? Rita Taylor?'

Susanna said, 'We need to follow both possibilities.'

'Yes,' said Blazeley. 'We do. And we need to find out what happened to Rita Taylor. Susanna, get Marion to put an action on HOLMES. Somebody visit 26 Canberra Drive and find out if whoever lives there now can tell us anything about her. If they can't, try the other houses in the street. Keep trying till someone remembers her. Twenty years is a long time, but it isn't for ever. There must be someone who hasn't moved away in that time.'

CHAPTER 22

That action on HOLMES was scheduled for the next day. When she saw the *Post* next morning, Susanna would wish they'd moved faster. Bernie Spence hadn't been part of the police discussions, but she'd come to the same conclusions about people to speak to. She wanted to learn as much as she could about Howard Diller's early years, but before then she wanted background information on Rita Taylor. A visit to the local registrar gave her the address at which Rita's birth had been registered. A check of the electoral roll told her that a woman with the surname Taylor still lived there. Bingo!

Bernie worked late into the night to make sure her story would be complete in time for the next day's first editions. Her editor signed it off as a front page lead, his only comments, "I love that bit about taking it lying down. I take it that was intentional? And the way you make it clear that Barry Humphries may have been the third man without inviting a law suit by actually saying so. You'll make it to the Street of Shame yet, Bernie."

A Mother's Lasting Grief

Bernadette Spence

Twenty years ago, sixteen-year-old Rita Taylor was raped by three men. Two of those men – lawyer Terence Carpenter and ex-teacher Michael Saville – have died in recent weeks in circumstances police describe as suspicious. Now, Rita's mother wonders whether someone is exacting revenge. Speaking exclusively to the *Post* from her home in Batterton, widowed Marjorie Taylor said, 'If they would do that to Rita, they would do it to others. Maybe one of those others has refused to take it lying down.'

Mrs Taylor says now that what she most regrets is that they didn't press charges against Carpenter, Saville and the third man at the time. 'We wanted what was best for Rita. My husband thought she should avoid publicity. Looking back, I'm not sure that was the best decision.' Her other regret is that she has lost touch with her daughter. She made it clear that her main reason for unburdening herself to this reporter was the hope that Rita might see the story and call her. What she wants more than anything is to get her daughter back. 'My husband, Rita's father, died four years ago. Rita wasn't at the funeral because I had no way to let her know. I'd like to hug her once more before I, too, am gone.'

Where Rita may be now, Mrs Taylor has no idea. 'Rita went to art school. She was very artistic. The last I heard, she was producing drawings for advertising agencies. But that was a long time ago.'

The name of the third man who raped Rita Taylor is not known, but sources say that the police are discounting the involvement of Howard Diller who hailed originally from Batterton and was killed in Kettering in circumstances closely resembling those surrounding Carpenter and Saville.

In unrelated news, police yesterday brought Barry Humphries before the magistrates on a charge of assault causing actual bodily harm. Unusually, the accused did not ask for bail and was remanded in custody. We have asked the police whether remand is to provide protection for Mr Humphries against some unidentified threat. No reply has been received as yet.

***

Deborah laid the newspaper down. 'They've got Barry Humphries's name. But not Ralph Townsend's'

'They've also got mine. And they are tying it to Carpenter and Saville.'

'But they don't know where you are.'

'And how long is that going to last? This damn journalist has talked to my mother. She's put it out there. Rita Taylor, artist, sells drawings to advertising agencies. It only needs one person at one agency to read that article and Bernadette Spence, may she rot in hell, will be round here.'

'How?'

'Well… Oh. Oh, Deborah. You little star. Rita Taylor hasn't sold a drawing since before she left art school. And I didn't live here then. When you told me to change my business name to Marie Fontaine, I thought it was just for the effect. You know… A more artistic name. But that wasn't the only reason. Was it?'

Deborah said, 'It certainly turned out to be a good idea. But Bernadette Spence is determined to be a pain in the hindquarters. If she keeps digging, she may find you in the end. Maybe we shouldn't wait for that to happen.'

'What do you mean?'

'We go to her before she comes to us. I call her. Using someone else's name. Hello, Bernie. I read your article, and so did Rita. Rita wants to meet you. Do you think she'll be able to refuse?'

Rita crossed the room, sat in Deborah's lap and pressed her cheek against Deborah's. 'You've got a plan. Haven't you, you clever, clever thing?'

'I think one may be emerging, my darling. It's

possible that Bernadette Spence's presence in the world is coming to an end.'

'Have we got enough morphine to do her and not have to forget about Ralph Townsend?'

'Oh, yes. Plenty.'

Rita giggled. 'I wonder how many people we'll have killed when it's all over?'

Deborah wriggled her nose against Rita's throat. 'That, my love, will depend on how many people stick their nose into things that are not their business.' She sat up. 'And what about your mother? She wants you to call her before she dies. Are you going to?'

'Not till hell freezes over. And probably not even then. She let me down.'

'She says she knows now they might not have made the right decision.'

'Now? What use is now? It was then I needed her. THEN. I don't need her now.'

***

That morning's briefing was dominated by Bernie Spence's column in the *Post* and it was downbeat. Bill Blazeley said, 'Whoever has the task of talking to Rita Taylor's mother, let's get it done.'

Rayyan said, 'Should we be giving the reporter a warning?'

'For what?' said Blazeley. 'Doing her job? Let's do ours as well as she does hers. Enough – what's done is done.'

'We could get the press office to speak to her,

though,' said Susanna. 'Nothing nasty – just, if she hears anything as a result of her article, will she please tell us as soon as possible. By which we would mean before she publishes it for the whole world to read.'

'Good idea,' said Blazeley. 'Except for the bit about the press office – I think we should do that ourselves. In fact, Susanna, I think you should do it. You may have to offer a little something in return.'

'Exclusivity when we catch the killers?'

'The other papers wouldn't stand for that. Give her something about Barry Humphries. No – better. Give her Ralph Townsend's name. But tell her she can't quote police sources.'

Rayyan said, 'Sir, shouldn't we be offering Townsend protection?'

'We probably should, Rayyan. Yes. But why don't we wait till he comes in here and asks for it? Because to do that, he has to admit to raping the girl. Otherwise, why would he be worried? Right. Other business. We have the initial toxicology reports on Terence Carpenter and Michael Saville. In both cases, their bloodstream contained strong traces of morphine. Not enough to kill them outright, but more than sufficient to incapacitate them. It will come as a great surprise if we don't find the same thing in Howard Diller's blood when that report comes in. It wasn't only morphine for Carpenter and Saville; the lab is working to isolate other components. And that brings me back to the very beginning and the murder of Terence Carpenter. Let's take a moment to think about that.

'He was dropped by a taxi at the end of Barracuda Street. The assumption is that he was on his way to Number 26, because that's where he always went. But he never got there. The assumption has to be that someone intercepted him – but no CCTV was pointing in that direction and no-one saw anything. I want that doublechecked. Marion, check the serial on the house-to-house in Barracuda Street. Was any address missed? Or any resident?'

Marion searched for the place in the incident log. She said, 'Three houses were empty at the time of the door-to-door. In four other houses, not all residents were home. Officers went back the following day and the day after that. The only house that wasn't signed off was number 24.'

'The one right next to the club?'

'I guess so, sir. Yes, that's how it looks. It was visited four times, but no-one was ever there.'

Blazeley said, '24 Barracuda Street. Who is it registered to?'

There was a pause while people scrabbled at keyboards and then a DC said, 'Samantha Corbyn, sir.'

'Sam Corbyn? The singer?'

'Looks like it, sir.'

'What do we know about her?'

Nicola said, 'She's a friend of my sister. Friends since school.'

'Have you met her?' asked Blazeley.

Nicola nodded. 'Once or twice. At parties – like that. She doesn't like parties much, though. In fact, I don't think she's wild about people. My sister told me, if Sam hasn't known you for thirty years, she probably doesn't want to. Keeps herself very private.'

'That can't be easy in a job like hers,' said Rayyan.

'The way I understand it,' said Nicola, 'you only see the real Sam if – well, as I said, if you've known her forever. She lives alone, isn't married, you see the pictures of her with men but it's all publicity. From what Sasha tells me, when the photographers have gone and Sam goes home, she goes home alone.'

'All right,' said Blazeley. 'Someone find out where Sam Corbyn is appearing right now.'

Another pause, and then a different DC said, 'She's been performing in Manchester. Started the day after Carpenter was killed and ended yesterday.'

'So she's probably back home now,' said Blazeley. 'Nicola, you've met her so you go and see her. Take Rayyan with you. Marion, make a note of that.'

'It's a longshot, sir,' said Rayyan. 'No one else saw anything. There's no reason to believe Sam Corbyn is any different. She may not even have been there.'

'Yes, Rayyan,' said Blazeley. 'It's a longshot.

Like most investigations. The majority of longshots lead nowhere. But there's always the exception. It's for the exception that we follow all of them up. The rest of you – we've reached that stage in the investigation where we have to reduce numbers. Some of you are being reassigned to other cases. DI David will tell you who is staying and who is going. Susanna, I'll be in my office.'

When he'd gone, Rayyan said, 'The DCI seems a bit down, boss.'

'It always gets that way, doesn't it?' said Susanna. 'The rush is over, we're down to the hard slog and no one knows when the breakthrough might come.' Or if, she thought. And will it come in time for me to buy a new dress for the wedding? Or am I going to let Chris down, first time out? She said, 'I'm going to let the reassigned officers know where they're going, and then I'll be trying to find Bernadette Spence. You two get off to Barracuda Street.'

'She's a singer, boss,' said Rayyan. 'A night bird. And she just got home, or at least we hope she did, after a series of gigs. Evening gigs. You don't think it's a bit early to be waking her up?'

'This is a murder enquiry,' said Susanna. 'It may well be a waste of time, as you so helpfully pointed out to the DCI with a complete disregard for your long term career, but it needs to be done and now is always better than later.'

**

214

Deborah had also been thinking about Bernadette Spence and next steps. She said to Rita, 'This meeting with the journalist. I've got a better idea.'

'Tell me?'

'What we talked about was that I tell her you want to talk to her. Get her to come here.'

'You're not so keen on that idea now?'

'Suppose she tells someone she's had that invitation? Or suppose, afterwards, someone listens to her messages? Or looks at her diary and finds she's written your name into it?'

Rita did a little shudder of the kind she knew turned Deborah on. 'We don't want that.'

'No. We don't. So here's an alternative. She mentions Howard Diller. I tell her that I knew Howard as a young man, and I can give her all the juicy facts a journalist wants.'

Rita put her arms around Deborah's neck. 'You are a genius.'

What Deborah did not add was that Bernadette Spence would not be the only person invited to their lair. She knew that if she waited for Rita to give her approval, Jamie Pearson would never join the growing list of the dead. And Jamie was a threat. Deborah believed in seeing things as they were – and she saw that Rita still carried a torch for Jamie. And Deborah hadn't been a mental health nurse without learning to recognise the signs that someone was not playing with a full deck. Deborah loved Rita. For Deborah, Rita was "The One." She knew that, if she analysed the love she felt, she would see that it had a great deal to do with Rita's vulnerability and need for protection allied with her own need to be a protector. So she didn't analyse it.

For her part, Rita was a great deal more aware than Deborah thought she was. She'd been with Deborah long enough and watched her closely enough, the way only those who really are vulnerable and know it ever watch people and do so for their own protection, that Deborah sometimes seemed to her an open book. She didn't know what Deborah was up to, but she knew she was up to something. She also knew that Deborah wasn't going to tell her what it was. And that could only mean that Rita wouldn't like it. For Rita, Deborah was not "The One." Deborah was "The One for Now." There's a difference.

Could anyone ever be "The One" for Rita? There was someone who had filled that position twenty years ago. He had failed when put to the test – but that did not mean he couldn't be invited to sit the test again.

Those feelings were Rita's most precious secret. She hugged them to herself. And she smiled. Deborah was familiar with that smile. To her, it was a sign of Rita's not being quite the full shilling. It was just as well that Deborah had chosen nursing instead of becoming a behavioural analyst. Her powers of analysis – of understanding – were less than perfect.

**

If Bernadette Spence was surprised to receive a visit from DI Susanna Howard, she took care not to let it show. 'Well, thank you, Inspector. I'm grateful for Ralph Townsend's name. But why are you giving it to me?'

'We aren't giving it to you, Bernie. If you ever suggest we did, we'll deny it.'

A smile touched the edges of Bernie's lips. 'Okay. So why are you not giving it to me?'

'It's what they call a quid pro quo.'

'Really? So in return for not giving me Ralph Townsend's name, you want me to… What?'

'Tell us – in fact, tell me – what you're planning to publish before you publish it.' She held up a hand to stop Bernie reacting immediately. 'Not so that we can prevent you. We won't try to do that. But so that we can react more effectively.'

The smile now affected far more than just the edges of Bernie's lips. Her beam could have lit a large room. She said, 'I outplayed you. Didn't I?'

Susanna took care to hide her irritation. 'I can see how you would think so.'

'How did you get Ralph Townsend's name?'

'From a witness who was there at the time. More than that, I can't say.'

'You don't need to, Inspector. There was more than one witness, but only one of them works for you. Only one is a police constable.'

'As I say, I can't tell you who gave us the name.'

'Have you talked to Townsend? Or do you plan to?'

'We have no plans to talk to him at the moment.'

'Okay. That tells me everything I need to know. You have a deal, Inspector. I'll tell you anything I'm about to publish before I publish it. But publish, I will.'

CHAPTER 23

Samantha Corbyn was in a deep sleep when Rayyan Padgett and Nicola Hayward knocked on her door. Her first reaction as she dragged herself from the dreamless depths was to ignore it. Whoever was there could not be anyone Samantha wanted to speak to. And, if they were, they could come back.

But the knocking did not stop. And then she heard someone shouting through her letterbox. 'Ms Corbyn. This is the police. We are outside your house and we really need to speak to you. Please open the door.'

She had gone to bed in a T-shirt and nothing else. She climbed out of it with the greatest reluctance and pulled on a baggy sweater and a pair of sweatpants. When she opened the door, Rayyan and Nicola were in no doubt that this visit was far from welcome. 'Yes? What do you want?' They held up their warrant cards and Rayyan introduced himself and Nicola. Sam Corbyn said, 'That tells me who you are. What I asked was what you want. I shouldn't be out of bed for at least another four hours.'

Rayyan said, 'May we come in, Ms Corbyn?'

She led the way to a very large kitchen, shouting, 'Shut the door behind you,' and switched on a coffee machine before emptying beans into a drum at the top. 'Sit down.'

Rayyan said, 'Ms Corbyn, would you mind telling us when you were last in this house before last night?'

'Why?'

'We are pursuing enquiries into the murder of a man called Terence Carpenter.'

Sam Corbyn nodded. 'I read about it. What has that to do with me?' She poured milk into a jug and warmed it with a wand from the coffee machine. Then she filled a cup with coffee and added some of the warm milk. She sat down at the island in the middle of the kitchen and took a deep draught of coffee. 'Forgive me. This time of day doesn't normally exist for me. If you want coffee, help yourselves. You can see where the cups are. I was last in this house a week ago last Thursday. I spent that night at the Midland Hotel in Manchester and the night just ending is the first since then that I've been anywhere else. What has that to do with a man being murdered?'

Rayyan looked downcast. 'Nothing, I'm afraid. A taxi dropped Mr Carpenter at the end of this street the day after you left for Manchester. We believe he was heading for the club next door. He never made it and you are the only person in the street we haven't been able to reach until now to ask if anyone saw anything. No one else did, and it's clear you couldn't have. I'm sorry to have troubled you.'

'I'm sorry, too, officer. I'm particularly sorry that you didn't have the sense, since you clearly know what I do for a living, to come in the afternoon. Nevertheless, even if I can't help you, I know someone who may be able to.' She finished her coffee and stood up. 'Come with me.'

The upstairs room overlooked the front garden and Barracuda Street. On a small stand resting on the windowsill was what looked like a very modern camera. Sam Corbyn patted it on the case. 'I call him Horace. He guards me against intrusion. A job like mine, you attract lots of fans and of course I like that – if I didn't have fans, I wouldn't sell tickets and I could end up stacking supermarket shelves because I don't have any other qualifications apart from my voice. And my physical attributes, of course, but I get the feeling that you've already clocked those, officer.' She looked towards Nicola, who had not been certain until this moment that Samantha had recognised her. 'Or, of course, I could do the sensible thing like Sasha and marry someone who worked in the City and made pots of money. Overall, I prefer being on my own and making my own living.'

Rayyan had turned bright red, conscious that he had indeed noticed that Sam Corbyn had not been short-changed in the upper body department. He said, 'You have this switched on all the time?'

'Every minute of every day. And it has everything. It should have – the whole package cost me more than twenty-five thousand pounds. There's another one just like it in a bedroom overlooking the back garden. It has infrared, so it sees in the dark. It's activated by movement, so if nothing happens in the street, it doesn't take any pictures. It focuses automatically, so wherever movement is taking place, Horace films it. That means I get an awful lot of recordings of cats pouncing on mice in the middle of the night, but I ignore those. What I'm looking for – why I bought the equipment – is a record of fans who carry fandom too far. Most fans are normal people, but some are a little obsessive and one or two are a menace.'

Nicola said, 'Where are the images stored?'

Sam Corbyn opened a cupboard and pointed to what looked something like a laptop. 'There. The very helpful man who installed this called that a server.' She stood back. 'When you're finished with it, I'd like it back, please. I feel naked without it and Horace relies on it one hundred percent. In fact, while you have it, I may as well turn him off. And now, if that's all, I'd like to get back to bed.'

When they were in Rayyan's car, the server in an evidence bag in Nicola's lap, she said, 'I always thought of her as a nice woman, and she is. Normally, we'd have to get a warrant before we could take the server. She just assumed we should have it.'

Rayyan nodded. 'Yes. Tremendously cooperative, considering we'd got her up at what for her must have seemed the crack of dawn.'

'And considering the way you were staring at her bosom, Sarge.'

Rayyan turned red once more. 'What are you talking about? There was no bosom to see. That sweater she was wearing was enormous.'

'Yes, Sarge. But then, it needed to be. And you couldn't tear your eyes away. But don't worry – I expect she's used to it.'

***

It didn't take Bernie Spence long to find out where Ralph Townsend lived, and with whom. She also knew how he earned his living. She'd learned early in her career that politeness and sensitivity were of little use to a journalist. Townsend was unlikely to be happy if she turned up at his door while his wife was there, but he would also have less room for manoeuvre. So that's what she did. When he opened the door, she said, 'Ralph Townsend? I'm Bernadette Spence from the *Post*. I'd like to talk to you about something that happened to a girl called Rita Taylor twenty years ago. I understand that you were there. May I come in?'

'No!'

He tried to close the door, but Bernie had already got her foot in the way. Her preferred footwear on jobs like this was Doc Martens – they resulted in less damage to her feet. She said, 'We've already published part of the story, Mr Townsend. Wouldn't you like to get your side out there, too?'

A woman had appeared behind Townsend. She

pushed him out of the way. 'I don't – yet – know what this is about, Ralph, but I do know I don't want the neighbours to hear it. Please come in, Ms Spence. The children are just getting ready for school. The bus will pick them up in five minutes, so any minute now they'll be out of here. I'd appreciate your not saying anything until they've gone. And then we can have a full and frank discussion.' She glanced at her husband. 'All three of us. Ralph, I suggest you ring the office and tell them you're going to be late.'

Forty minutes later, when Bernie Spence left the Townsend home, Ralph Townsend was ringing his office again – this time to say that he wouldn't be coming in at all that day. His wife had just discovered that her husband as a young man had participated in the rape of an underage girl, that the police would inevitably become aware of it as part of other investigations they were pursuing, that Ralph was likely to be charged and that the Post would be giving the story a great deal of publicity, starting with hints to be published that day. Their neighbours would see those hints and they would interpret them. So would the parents of their children's schoolmates. There was every likelihood that Ralph would receive a prison sentence. The Townsends had a great deal to talk about.

Bernie asked herself, as she had done many times in the past, whether she felt any guilt about building her career on outcomes like this. The answer was: No. People did what they did. They made the mistakes they made and took the risks they took. Ralph had been a much younger man and single when he did what he did to Rita, and it was clear from his wife's reaction that he'd been a very different person then. She had been astonished that the Ralph Townsend she knew could ever have been capable of such an action. Be that as it may, it had been a matter of choice. No one had forced him to do what he did. If mercy was to be shown him, that would be a matter for the sentencing judge. It wasn't something Bernie had to think about.

CHAPTER 24

Susanna gave the task of playing through the film from the camera known as Horace to two detective constables. She told them the day and the approximate time they were looking for and showed them a photograph of Terence Carpenter, although they were working on the murder team and already familiar with what Carpenter looked like. 'As soon as you see Carpenter appear on the film, pause it right there and call me.'

It took longer than it might have done because the DCs first had to learn how to use the playback equipment, which predated anything they were used to, and then had to work out how to match date and time to places on the film, but eventually they called Susanna. She asked Blazeley, Rayyan and Nicola to join her. The DCs played the relevant piece of tape for them.

The action could not have been clearer. Terence Carpenter walked down Barracuda Street until stopped by a woman. Another woman was standing just behind her. Blazeley said, 'Stop it right there. Blow that up as far as you can. I want to see what that is she's holding in her hand.'

It was a balancing act, because getting the image large enough to see the object clearly meant that it became impossible to read, but none of the four officers was in much doubt about what they were looking at. 'It's a warrant card,' said Rayyan.

'Or it's meant to look like one,' said Susanna. 'And Howard Diller's killers, let us remember, pretended to be interviewing him as police officers.'

'Carry on running the tape,' said Blazeley. And they watched Terence Carpenter first expostulating before giving up with a shrug and going with the two women to a car. He got into the back seat, they got into the front, and the car drove away.

Susanna said, 'That's how they got him. He thought he was being taken in for questioning. They took him back to his place and they killed him. But did you notice how they kept their heads down?'

Blazeley nodded. 'There's no way we're going to get a recognisable print of either of them off that tape. But at least that's one more "don't know" ticked off. We know how he was picked up and we've confirmed it was two women.'

Rayyan said, 'But what a palaver!'

'Yes,' said Nicola. 'Why wait till he was out in the street? Why take that risk? Why not just walk up to his front door, hold up your fake warrant cards and say, "May we come in?" I don't get it.'

'Theatre,' said Blazeley. 'One of the women was putting on a show for the other one. Think about it – the two of them are going around killing people and in Howard Diller's case they showed they didn't need a reason – Diller had done nothing, but they killed him. These two don't live

227

in the same world as the rest of us. Things have to be done for show. They live their lives on a stage. It's what makes reality TV so popular.'

'Ah,' said Nicola. 'I had wondered what could do that.'

'Unfortunately,' said Susanna, 'we only see the car from the side. We can tell the make and the colour – it's a dark blue Renault – but we don't have the number. Let's get Marion to list a new action to identify every dark blue Renault in Batterton. Then let's get someone working on it.

***

While MCIT were playing their cerebral games in an attempt to outwit two killers, Jamie Pearson and Theresa McErlane had more mundane things to deal with. Control Room had sent them to a row of shops where a caller had reported a robbery in progress. Since they were only two streets away, there was every chance they would catch the robbers in the act. Jamie turned on the flashing lights and drove with his foot on the floor. When they got there, they saw a man emerging from an off-licence clutching a bag and with a wild expression on his face.

Jamie said, 'He might as well be wearing a striped jersey and a mask and carrying a bag marked "Swag." But he was talking to himself, because Theresa was out of the car and chasing the thief into an alley at the side of the off-licence. By the time Jamie had stopped the car and followed her, she had reached a wall at the end of the alley the robber was about to climb over, grabbed his ankle and hauled him back.

The robber was not about to be taken without a fight. He held a knife and the knife had traces of blood on it. Now Jamie faced a dilemma. The policeman's duty is – always – to preserve life before anything else, and the blood on that knife suggested that the robber had inflicted a potentially life-ending injury on someone in the off-licence. Jamie knew he should check that out immediately. But the knife was now in his partner's face and every trace of what he saw as his youthful failure told him he could not desert her.

The robber was advancing towards Theresa. Theresa was not backing away. The look on the robber's eye said, "This is not an act." He reached out the hand without the knife in an attempt to grab Theresa by the neck, and Jamie pulled his telescopic baton from its sheath and brought it down hard on the robber's other arm. The knife fell to the ground, Jamie kicked it away, seized the robber's other arm and slammed him to the ground. He shouted, 'There's blood on that knife. Check the offy.' As Theresa ran back up the alley, Jamie rolled the robber onto his face, handcuffed him and told him he was under arrest.

Even handcuffed, the robber made it difficult for Jamie to force him up the alley towards the car. As he passed the off-licence, Theresa shouted,

'The manager has been knifed. He's bleeding buckets. I've called for backup. An ambulance is on its way.'

It was an hour before Jamie and Theresa reached the police station and the custody suite. Jamie said, 'Book him in.'

'Don't you want to do it? You arrested him.'

'When you're in Major Crimes, I want you to have something to remember about the lives us poor foot soldiers lead. Book him in.'

Theresa stared at him for a moment, and then pushed the prisoner in front of the custody sergeant who said, 'What have we here?'

'PC Pearson arrested this man for Section 18 GBH and assault on an emergency worker.'

'Circumstances, please?'

Theresa said, 'We were called to a robbery in action at an off-licence in Mandela Way. When we got there, we found the off-licence manager semi-conscious and bleeding from stab wounds. The prisoner tried to escape and was in possession of a knife covered in blood. He then went to grab me and threatened me with the knife.'

The custody sergeant said to the robber, 'Do you understand why you've been arrested?' When the robber simply stared at her she said, 'You have been brought here for questioning in regard to offences involving robbery, assaulting an officer and the use of a knife. I'm going to authorise your detention to secure and preserve evidence and obtain evidence by questioning. Do you understand?' When there was still no answer from the robber, she said, 'Give me your name.'

'Fred Fanakapan,' said the robber.

'Most amusing,' said the sergeant. 'Take the handcuffs off him. I'll book you as Refused all Details for now, sir. Search him, please.'

When he had been photographed standing against a chart that indicated his height, his fingerprints were taken and checked against the database. This told the custody sergeant that the robber was neither Refused all Details nor Fred Fanakapan but Billy Mitchell. The sergeant said, 'According to the database, Billy, we last took your prints eight years ago. When I check, will I find you've been banged up for most of that time?'

'I just got out,' said Billy.

'And now you're just going back in,' said the sergeant. 'You must like being inside. Is it the food that attracts you? In any case, would you like a copy of the code of practice that tells you what you should expect and what you are entitled to while you are in custody?'

'Don't be ridiculous,' said Billy.

'There have been some changes in eight years, Billy.'

'I don't want to see your code of practice. All right?'

Theresa and Jamie left them and went for a cup of tea in the canteen. When they were sitting down, Theresa said, 'How did you know I want to get into Major Crimes?'

'Oh, Theresa. It's written all over you. It's in everything you do. And good luck to you. It's never appealed to me, but I understand the attraction.'

Theresa was looking at him in a way she hadn't looked at him before. 'You're a hero.'

'I did my job, Theresa. Just like you did yours.'

'He had me outgunned.'

'No, he didn't. If I hadn't used the baton, you would have. Anyway, I was backing up a colleague. You'd do exactly the same. That's what we do. I get your back and you get mine.'

There were other people in the canteen. One or two had heard about her arrest and stopped by their table to congratulate her. Uniformed officers arrest people regularly – it's part of their job – but a GBH and possible murder was special. Theresa enjoyed the attention, but the presence of all these people was a problem, because what she really wanted to do was to reward Jamie with a kiss. She wasn't going to do that here in front of everyone, but as soon as the opportunity presented itself, she intended to take it. It wasn't completely out of the question that she might encourage him to take down her particulars.

***

Susanna was also bent on taking an opportunity, in this case to talk to Superintendent McAvoy. She said, 'We've reached that stage where the number of people on the case is reduced and we battle on, looking for the lead that will give us a breakthrough. Am I being too optimistic if I say that means I think I can take the wedding weekend off?'

McAvoy smiled. 'I don't think you're being too optimistic at all. And make sure you take the whole weekend, because that's what I'll be doing. We'll get there on the Friday evening and we won't leave until sometime on the Sunday.'

'Great, Chris. But…'

'Yes, I sensed there was going to be a "but." What is it?'

'I want to be a credit to you.'

'You couldn't be anything else.'

'It's nice of you to say so. But the women at this wedding, and especially Maria since she is Paula's sister, are going to be looking at the clothes people wear. And women can be a little more demanding about clothes than men. Particularly about the clothes worn by the woman who is coming with the man who, until she died, was married to her sister.'

McAvoy's smile had become broader. 'Have you made some plan I haven't heard of? Are you going in fancy dress?'

'Chris. The weekend we found out that Terence Carpenter had got himself murdered, my plan was to find a new dress for the occasion. I was going to spend the whole of Saturday doing that, which would give me enough time to have something taken in or let out if I couldn't find exactly the right size. But Terence Carpenter did get himself murdered, and we did find out...'

'And that put an end to any clothes shopping.'

'Exactly.'

'Why don't you tell Blazeley you need tomorrow off? Don't tell him why – just say it's personal.'

'He'll object.'

'No, he won't. As you said, this is the stage the enquiry has reached, and Bill has had plenty of experience of that. He knows personal things come up, even for coppers. And I'll tell you what; I'll take tomorrow off, too, and we'll look for that dress together.'

'Did you ever go shopping for her clothes with Paula?'

'Yes. I did. And I did exactly what I'm planning to do with you tomorrow – sit on a chair and agree with you. And have lunch together. And generally dawdle around town. And enjoy your company.'

* * *

Having left Ralph Townsend and his wife mulling over their future, and whether they had one together, Bernie now had the bones of the next story she was going to write. But she wasn't done yet. There was a message on her phone to say that someone who had read her reference to Howard Diller wanted to talk to her about Howard as a young man. "I can tell you," the message said, "what it was Diller did that upset his parents so badly they cut him out of their lives." Bernie rang the number the caller had left. Some nice juicy titbits of the sort Howard Diller's parents had not been prepared to provide would get her another front-page lead.

No cop receiving a message like that would respond to it without backup. But Bernie was a journalist, not a cop, and keeping things to herself till the cat was in the bag was second nature.

CHAPTER 25

Jamie Pearson had also received an invitation; in his case, to an old school reunion. He told Theresa McErlane and she was pleased for him. But a little concerned. They were parked by the side of the road, waiting for the next call. It had been a quiet night. Theresa said, 'You don't talk about your school days. Did you enjoy them?'

'Enjoy? Yes. No. Well, sometimes. It was school, you know? It had its moments.'

'I certainly know that school. It's the same one I went to. A few years later, of course. Is that where you met Rita?'

Jamie was silent for a little while and Theresa wondered whether she'd made a mistake by mentioning that name. Then he said, quietly, 'Yes. That's where I met Rita.'

'And the people you meet at this reunion. They'll remember Rita? And what happened to her?'

Jamie nodded. 'Yes. Yes, I suppose they will.'

Theresa let the silence run for a while. Then she said, 'This guy who's invited you. The one organising the reunion. What's his name?'

'Tulley. Bill Tulley.'

'Was he a close friend of yours?'

'Close? Bill? No, I wouldn't call him close. We knew each other but we weren't in the same circle. He didn't live near me, and we had different interests. Really, I was surprised that Bill would be the one to organise a reunion. He always seemed like he wanted to finish school and get on with his life.'

'Do you know what happened to him?'

'No idea. As I said, we weren't in the same circle. I never heard another word from him or about him till now.'

'I wonder how he got your address?'

'No idea.'

'Are you in touch with anybody else you were at school with?'

'Am I? I don't think I am. I ended up a bit like Bill, wanting to put it all behind me.'

'Was that the Rita business, do you think?'

Jamie's silence this time was even longer than it had been before. 'Yes,' he said eventually. 'I suppose it was. I felt so ashamed... And then, you know, I threw everything into my police training. And I don't think the other people at school thought very much of someone joining the police.'

'No,' said Theresa. 'I've had exactly the same experience. I know people I was at school with had a reunion recently, and I wasn't invited. And I didn't mind one little bit. I don't know what it is – that school doesn't produce criminals to any greater extent than any other school, but somehow the kids look on us as... Well, not enemies exactly... But not as being on their side. Not friends. I suppose that's why I'm being so nebby. I'm wondering why you've been invited. Will you go?'

'Well… Yes. Probably. I mean, yes, I will. It's tomorrow. In the evening. Which will be very convenient because this is our last nightshift – we're back on days after tomorrow.'

'Really? That soon? Usually, reunions are planned way in advance.'

'I suppose they must be. Obviously, including me was an afterthought. It won't be a great big thing with partners I've never met, because the invite made it clear they weren't included.'

'No partners? It actually said that?'

'Yes. It did. Is that unusual? I wouldn't know; I've never been invited to a reunion before.'

The concern Theresa felt was increasing by the minute. 'I think it is unusual, Jamie. Yes. Usually, they invite you to take along your significant other.'

'Well, not this time.'

Theresa would have liked to explore this further, but they got a call to a three-car collision on the bypass and that put an end to conversation for some time.

***

Deborah smiled as she let Bernadette Spence into the house. 'Are you okay to climb stairs? Only, we'd like to have this chat on the top floor.'

Bernie felt as though she'd just been insulted. Okay to climb stairs? Did she look like some doddering oldie? She was a damn sight younger than this woman – fitter, too, she wouldn't mind betting. 'Yes,' she said, trying to keep coldness out of her voice because she did, after all, want something from the woman. 'I'm sure I'll be able to climb whatever stairs you have to offer.' And she set off in front of Deborah, bent on showing just how quickly she could climb.

When she reached the top, the stairs opened into a single enormous room that was filled with light from a ceiling that seemed to be nothing but glass. In the room were an easel, a bed, a small fridge and two chairs, in one of which a woman who looked in her mid thirties was sitting. The chairs were on what looked like a tarpaulin. The woman treated Bernie to a smile of immense sweetness. 'Hello, Bernadette,' she said. 'My name is Rita Taylor. I believe you've been looking for me.'

And then Bernie felt an enormous shock wave passing through her, and she fell to the floor. When she came to, she was sitting in one of the chairs, around the back of which her arms were secured by something that allowed almost no movement at all. The woman who had introduced herself as Rita Taylor was standing right in front of her, her face close to Bernadette's and her eyes staring into Bernie's own. She said, 'We're going to leave you here for a while, Bernie. Is it all right if I call you Bernie? It may be a short while and it may be days. We'll decide. You'll probably wet yourself while you wait – the last person we kept waiting did. That's why we put the tarp down. We live here, after all. And this is my studio. Apart from wetting yourself, what we want you to do while you're waiting for us to come back is to meditate. The subject of your meditation should be the wisdom – or the lack of it – of sticking your nose into other people's business.

'You'll probably want to shout for help, but I would be cautious about that, if I were you. In the first place, we are far enough from the neighbours that no-one will hear you. No-one outside, that is. But we will hear you, Bernie, and my partner may become irritated. You don't want to irritate my partner, Bernie. She's already given you one blast from her taser, and that was without being annoyed at all. Think what she might do if she really gets cross with you.'

With that, Rita moved her face even closer to Bernie's and kissed her gently on the lips. 'We'll be back.' She opened Bernie's bag and removed the phone from it. 'And we'll take this with us.'

While Rita had been talking, Deborah had moved the easel so that it stood directly in Bernie's line of sight. Then Rita and Deborah left the room and Bernie heard them walking down the stairs. She looked at the easel, not out of curiosity but because the way she and it were positioned made it impossible not to. Three drawings were arranged for her to see. Even in her befuddled state, the quality of the draughtsmanship was clear. But the subject matter made her blood run cold.

Next day, Theresa McErlane had a day off in preparation for the switch back to days. She had a number of things she wanted to do with it, and they took her back to school. The school she had attended and Jamie Pearson had been to some years before her. Although she wasn't working that day, she went in uniform. The school secretary seemed delighted to see her. 'Theresa! It seems like forever! My, don't you look something in your uniform? Is this a social visit? Or are you here officially?'

Theresa sat on a chair in front of the secretary's desk. She leaned forward, conspiratorially, like someone about to impart a secret. 'It's sort of official, Mrs Jerome – but it has to remain completely confidential. At least for now. Actually, it isn't official at all – I'm trying to do a favour for a colleague of mine. Jamie Pearson.'

'Oh, I certainly remember Jamie. In fact, I see him around town from time to time.' She snapped her fingers. 'And I saw you with him! You were driving and he was beside you.'

Theresa beamed, eager to show how pleased she was but in reality reinforcing the unofficial, social aspect of the visit. 'That's right! Jamie was assigned as my mentor. He's been terrific. I'll be moving on soon, probably into Major Crimes Investigation, and I want to do something to thank him. But I don't want anyone to know until after it happens.'

The secretary tapped one finger against the side of her nose. 'Mum's the word. You can rely on me; I won't tell a soul.' She leaned forward in her turn, so that their two heads were now only inches apart. 'What do you want to know?'

'Bill Tulley,' said Theresa. 'Do you know if he still lives in town?'

'Bill Tulley. Bill Tulley.' She was wrapping her fingers against her head, deep in thought. Then, 'I remember! He was a few years before you.'

'Yes. He was in the same year as Jamie.'

'That's right! Let's have a look now.' She moved her mouse around and clicked on a few keys. 'We try to keep up to date with our ex-pupils. The way budgets are now, sometimes the only way we can get the things the school needs is if the public chips in. It's mostly parents who contribute, of course, but we do make appeals from time to time. Well, I expect you know that – you've probably had one yourself.'

'Not yet,' said Theresa. 'But I'm sure my time will come.'

'You can count on it, my dear. Anyway... Bill Tulley... No, Bill doesn't still live here. Far from it. He emigrated to Australia. Were you hoping to put the two of them in touch?'

'Not just Bill – I picked his name because I've heard Jamie talk about him from time to time. What I'd really like to do is arrange a little party for Jamie with people he was at school with.'

'A reunion! What a lovely idea. People hold

them from time to time – they usually tell us about it so that we can put something in the school newsletter.'

'Do they? Have you heard about any reunions happening around about now?'

Mrs Jerome shook her head. 'No. The last one was just before Christmas, a few months ago now. Listen, would you like me to give you a little list of two or three people who were quite close to Jamie when he was here? You can contact them and see what other names they can suggest.'

'Would you? That would be so helpful. And how about Bill Tulley? Could you possibly give me the names of three people he wouldn't have wanted a reunion without?' And when she left ten minutes later, Theresa had in her tablet the names and addresses of three former pupils without whom, Mrs Jerome assured her, Jamie would never consider a reunion to be complete. She ignored that list. If she ever contacted them, it might be to invite them to a wedding. But the three close friends of Bill Tulley were another matter. She called on each one of them, still in uniform, and asked a simple question: Have you been invited to a school reunion tomorrow? None of them had.

***

Susanna's request for a day off had met with less resistance than she had expected. 'Sure,' Blazeley had said. 'Give yourself a break. Recharge your batteries. I know we like to stick to this idea that nobody has any time of their own while a murder enquiry is going on, but I think that's counter-productive. You become exhausted and you miss things. Whatever it is you want to do tomorrow, go and do it. You'll come back the next day in much better shape. And I'll be watching over the team while you're away.'

For Chris McAvoy, getting the day off had been a lot easier. He had simply informed the Detective Chief Superintendent that he was taking it.

And so they had started the day in bed together. Then Chris had got up, showered and gone downstairs to make breakfast. Susanna followed him into the shower before dressing and following the scent of bacon and black pudding frying to the kitchen. Two full English breakfasts, a large pot of tea and quite a lot of toast and they were ready. Susanna said, 'I hope I find what I'm looking for. There won't be another chance before the wedding.'

'I have no doubt at all that the day is going to be a great success. I'll drive. You think about dresses.'

***

Nicola felt guilty when she saw her sister's name on her phone's screen. She knew she was supposed at least to have touched base since cancelling their dinner engagement and she simply hadn't had time. And that, of course, was never true – the fact was, she hadn't made time. It need only have taken a minute.

But Sasha didn't seem to be cross with her. 'This doggy bag. I'm telling you, the food was so fantastic I've had to force myself not to dig into it. And if you don't get round here by lunchtime, I will stop forcing myself. I'm at home right now; I'll be here till two. After that – well, you've no idea what you'll be missing.'

'Sasha, I'm so sorry. This is my first murder and you've no idea how busy we've been. I'm going to duck out of here for two hours. See you soon.'

When she reached Sasha's house, the contents of the doggy bag were laid out on plates. 'Help yourself,' said Sasha. 'Call it lunch. If you take it home for later, you know your lodger is going to ruin your enjoyment by staring at you in envy. So eat it now.'

And Nicola had done just that. Between bites, she said, 'How did our mother react when you told her I'd missed George Clooney?'

'She wasn't best pleased. But you know what she thinks.'

'I do. I'm wasting my time, wasting my life and wasting my opportunities. What I should be doing is what she did and you did – finding a chap with big earning potential and wrapping myself around him.'

'Is that what I did?' asked Sasha. 'It didn't feel like that. I thought I was in love. Still do, actually.'

245

'Yes, yes, but you know what I mean. Our mother would say it's as easy to fall in love with a man with pots of money as it is to fall for a pauper – so why even consider the pauper?'

'Are you? Considering a pauper? Is there some penniless man in your life that none of us have heard about?'

Nicola laughed. 'There's no man in my life, penniless or otherwise. And that's what she finds reprehensible. Yes, she does,' she said, holding up a hand as Sasha seemed about to respond. 'She thinks being on your own is wrong for a woman. And she may be right – perhaps someone in my life is what I do need to make it complete. But…' The memory of the interview with Jenny McMurtry, the woman in Terence Carpenter's short-lived and disastrous marriage came back to her. 'We interviewed someone recently, me and Rayyan. A woman. You know what she told us? That she hadn't married her present husband to irritate her father, but the fact that he would be irritated was a bonus. I've got some sympathy with that idea. If you have any influence with our mother, get her to ease off about me and men.'

'I'll do my best. I have no more influence with her than you do, but I'll try what gentle hints can do.'

'Well, I can answer that for you. Gentle hints have no effect whatsoever on Mummy.' She finished the last goody on the last plate. 'But I am very sorry I missed that dinner. If what I've just eaten is any guide, it would very likely have been the best meal I've ever eaten.'

* * *

Theresa McErlane was in the women's locker room, changing out of her uniform, when another WPC spoke to her. 'Any progress with Jamie?'

Theresa looked at her. 'What?'

'Jamie Pearson. Your mentor. Are you getting anywhere with him?'

Bewildered, Theresa said, 'Well. I did my driving courses before I was partnered with him. And most of the rest I learned at training school.'

'Theresa! Are you being deliberately thick? I'm not talking about the job. Or, if I am, I'm talking about being on the job. Have you let him... Well, let's not get too personal, but... A kiss, perhaps? Holding hands? Going round his on your day off? Don't be obtuse. Have you made it to first base yet?'

'What the hell are you talking about? Me and Jamie? Whatever makes you think...'

'Oh, Theresa. The whole shift is talking about it. We only have to look at the expression on your face when he's around. But he hasn't cottoned on yet, has he? I suppose that's why he's still single at his age. You'll have to take it on yourself. Anyway, I'm done here. See you tomorrow.'

After she'd gone, Theresa stood for some time looking at the door she'd left through. Was that what people thought? And were they right?

247

And she knew, with the strangest combination of a sinking and a rising heart: they were.

CHAPTER 26

The editor at the *Post* was not in the best of moods. He'd kept space open on the front page of the afternoon edition for as long as he dared because Bernadette Spence had assured him she was on the trail of what she called "a biggie." She had promised to be in touch by midday at the latest, but midday had come and gone and the editor had had to fill the space with some drivel from a council press release about the need to obtain approval for the chopping down of plane trees that had lined a set of streets for more than a hundred years. That was no substitute for what Bernie had promised.

And if he dug a little deeper, he knew that it was not just the empty front page space that was bothering him. Bernie was on a story. The story already had three murders in it. It needed to be approached with a degree of caution. And the editor knew that caution was completely alien to Bernie Spence. So he had better exercise some for her. He called the police and asked to speak to Susanna David. Told that she was not there, he asked for Nicola Hayward, but Nicola was just finishing her impromptu lunch with her sister. He left a message asking her to call him sooner rather than later.

That message was not at this point put onto HOLMES because there was no reason to connect it with the murders. That changed when Nicola, receiving the message, went straight to the newspaper office instead of back to the police station. She listened to the editor with respectful attention. 'Do you know who she was planning to talk to?'

'No! That's the problem. All our reporters are supposed to file a day plan at the start of each day. If that changes, which it will because leads and contacts are coming in all the time, they are supposed to update the plan. None of them is very good at doing that, and Bernie is worst of all. You have to understand, officer; ambitious journalists live by their latest story. There's no honour among them – if another reporter realised what Bernie was after and thought they could get it faster, they'd steal it without a moment's hesitation. So reporters tend to keep anything meaty to themselves. If she was doing a Townswomen's Guild meeting or some am dram production, she'd let anyone know who wanted to, because who's going to want to steal that? But Bernadette Spence outgrew Townswomen's Guild and amateur dramatics some time ago.'

'All right. So you don't know what she was doing, but you're worried enough to call the police. That means you suspect she was going to see someone and the idea makes you fearful. Who?'

'I think she was getting close to Rita Taylor.'

'Would that be a bad thing? Do you have any reason to suppose that Rita Taylor is dangerous?'

'Bernie thinks Rita may be the one who's bumping people off. She may be the killer. Are you going to tell me that that thought hasn't entered the minds of the police?'

Nicola had to be careful how she handled that. She only had the editor's word that Bernie Spence was missing. The woman might be sitting in a nearby office, just waiting for police confirmation to run a story that Rita Taylor was a prime suspect. On the other hand, she might, as the editor said, be missing and, as the editor feared, in serious danger. Police training means that the first duty of any officer, even outweighing the duty to apprehend offenders, is to preserve life. She decided to ignore the question. 'I take it you've tried her mobile.'

'Yes, I have. There's no answer.'

'Is that unusual?'

The editor almost broke into a smile. 'No. Of course it isn't unusual. The bloody woman never responds to a call or message unless she chooses to. And if she's keeping watch on someone, she'll as like as not turn it off so that the ringing doesn't disturb whoever she's watching. Look, now that I start to think about it, I've probably been worrying too much. Chances are she's going to walk in here sometime soon with the story I've been waiting for. Or, if it's as big a story as she was hoping for, she might even be on the phone to one of the nationals right now bargaining for a job.'

'She wants to leave you?'

'Every journalist at her stage of development wants to work for a national. It's why you become a reporter. I was like that myself at one time.'

'But she'll have got this story on time you were paying her for.'

'I wish I believed that would make a difference. Look, I've got this off my chest now. Why don't we do this? We'll leave it for now. If she does turn up, I promise to let you know. If she still isn't here at this time tomorrow, that'll be soon enough to worry. Okay?'

'Okay. If you're sure. But give me a picture of her if you have one, just in case.'

'Oh, we have one all right – a big enough story and Bernie will want her photograph on her byline.'

And Nicola left the newspaper offices. But she wasn't swayed by the reduction in the editor's level of worry. When she got back to the police station, she asked Marion to enter into HOLMES Bernie Spence's possible disappearance and the fact that she may be in contact with Rita Taylor. Then she asked Control Room to transmit Bernie's photograph and details to all officers with a request that Nicola Hayward be advised if anyone caught sight of the reporter.

***

One of the people who received that request was Susanna David. She was sitting in a restaurant with Chris McAvoy having just enjoyed the most relaxed meal she'd eaten since news had come in that Terence Carpenter had been murdered. On the floor beside her were a number of bags. One of them contained a dress that she thought would be perfect for the wedding. She had also bought some rather expensive underwear and was about to suggest to Chris that they go home so she could model it for him when she saw the notification. She said, 'Excuse me a moment,' to Chris and rang Nicola. 'Tell me about the missing reporter.'

'She may not be missing, boss,' said Nicola. 'The editor can't make up his mind. I might not have made a fuss of it if her boss hadn't said that she was getting close to Rita Taylor and she thought – well, you know what she thought. She thought what we think.'

'That these murders may be revenge for the rape of Rita and that Rita may be one of the killers.'

'Exactly.'

'And she hasn't let anyone know where she's going? She's deliberately walked into what could be a death trap without any backup?'

'Apparently, that's what reporters do. She didn't tell anyone else because she doesn't want anyone to steal the story.'

'We need to find Rita Taylor, Nicola.'

'We're doing what we can, boss. DCI Blazeley has got eight people contacting advertising agencies all over the country asking if any of them have had work done by Rita Taylor at any time in the recent past. He also sent a DC to her mother to collect a photograph. We're having it updated to what she probably looks like now, and every officer will get a copy. He's thinking about giving it to the press and television, as well. If anything comes of either of those things, I'll make sure you're informed. In the meantime, enjoy your day off – you'll be back here tomorrow.'

'How are we getting on with the search for a dark blue Renault?'

Nicola laughed. 'There are a lot of them registered in and around Batterton and none to a Rita Taylor. There's a small army of PCs, each armed with the picture of what Rita Taylor probably looks like now, out there ticking them off one by one. If we don't get lucky with an early strike, it could be a month before we've checked them all.'

'That's good advice,' said Chris when she told him about the conversation. 'Blazeley is a good man. He'll see it through without you being there. What do you want to do next?'

She looked at him, wondering whether he sensed what might be in her mind. Then she said, 'Let's go home.' It pleased her that she had finally begun to think of Chris's place as home. She said, 'Do you think it's time for me to move more of my stuff into your place?'

'Oh, Susanna, I do. I so do.'

***

Deborah said, 'What do you suppose the police are doing right now?'

'I've no idea. Well, yes I have – they'll be looking for our guest. They won't find her, though, will they?'

'Would you like to know what I think they're doing? I mean, apart from that?'

'Yes. Of course I would.'

'I think they are contacting all the firms they think Rita Taylor might have done any work for and asking where they can find you.'

'And they'll draw a blank.' She giggled. 'It's funny, isn't it? What are we going to do about our guest?'

'I think we should let her suffer for a while. Maybe keep her alive till the day after tomorrow.'

'Not tomorrow?'

'No, my love, because you will want to be there when we do it so that you can draw it afterwards, and I've got something I need you to do tomorrow.'

'What? What do you need me to do?'

'I want you to take her phone and drive it way up north. Edinburgh, probably. And I want you to come back the next day without it.'

'Why? Why can't we do it together? Why do we need to do it at all? Why, Deborah?'

'Because the police will be getting the phone company to monitor it. That's what they do. By tomorrow, the phone company will start telling them where it is.'

'So they'll be telling them where Bernadette Spence is?'

'Where they think she is. That's exactly right. And they'll head off up to Scotland looking for her.'

'But she won't be there.'

'That's right, because she'll be here. We'll make sure you have plenty of money. Leave the phone in a litter bin in Scotland, book yourself into a hotel, then set off next morning, come back here, and we'll put an end to the interfering Bernadette Spence. And then we'll see about doing the same to Ralph Townsend.'

'And that will be that. The end of the killings. No more.'

'No more killings. If that's what you want, that's what you shall have. You know how I feel about Jamie Pearson…'

'And you know how I feel about him…'

'And you'll be the one who has her way. No more killings after the reporter and Ralph Townsend.'

'Promise?'

'Cross my heart and hope to die.'

***

Rita wasn't fooled. It made her sad, but she knew her lover was lying. She'd suspected for a while that Deborah was plotting something, and now she was certain. Well, she would let Deborah believe she was going along with the act.

What she would not do was drive to Scotland with Bernadette Spence's phone. Oh, she'd leave the house as though she were going to do what Deborah asked – but she wouldn't go far. She'd dump the reporter's phone, if that would keep the police away from the house. But after that she'd have the house under observation. If Deborah went anywhere, Rita would know. And she would follow her.

And if anyone came to the house, she'd know that, too.

CHAPTER 27

Next day, Jamie had gone back to his state of worrying without saying what he was worrying about and Theresa had had enough. 'Jamie. You would try the patience of a saint. And I'm not one. Will you please tell me what the hell has got into you now?'

Jamie was staring into space. 'This dark blue Renault we're all supposed to be looking for.'

'Yes! What about it?'

'And this photograph of a woman. When we check places with dark blue Renaults, we're supposed to make sure that she doesn't live there. And if she does, we have to tell MCIT immediately.'

'Yes! You still haven't explained… Oh, no. Oh, Jamie. Tell me it isn't.'

'But that's the point. It is. This picture has been doctored to say what she looks like now. But that doesn't change the fact…'

When it seemed he wouldn't or couldn't finish the sentence, Theresa said, 'You think that's Rita. Don't you?'

'It's not a question of what I think, Theresa. It is her.'

'So you think… You think MCIT want to speak to Rita about multiple murders. Is that what you think?'

'Isn't it what I always thought? Didn't I say this

right at the start? Rita is taking her revenge. Another woman is helping her, but these murders are about Rita. Rita is a killer.'

Theresa let the information sink in. She was so aware of wanting to hug the poor, tormented man beside her in the car. She said, 'Look. We've only been assigned ten of these index numbers to check so even if one of the dark blue Renaults in Batterton does belong to Rita, and that's far from certain, there isn't much likelihood that it will be you and me that find her. But here's what we do. We make checking our ten the priority. Unless we get a call to a scene somewhere, we check the Renaults before we do anything else. That way, they'll all be done and you can relax.'

'Relax? Relax! How am I supposed to relax, knowing that Rita is wanted for questioning for murder?'

Theresa thought about what she was going to say, and whether she should say it. It was time. She knew that. Jamie needed to face up to the fact that he was devoted to a fantasy. And she needed to let her feelings be known. She said, 'Jamie. I'm sorry, but I have to say this. I'm really sorry that you've gone through what you've gone through over Rita. I'm sorry you still beat yourself up because at the age of sixteen you weren't able to take on three grown men, even though they'd probably have beaten the shit out of you. I'm sorry you think that you were the one who did wrong, when it's blindingly obvious to anyone that you have nothing to reproach yourself for and the guilty parties are now paying the ultimate price. I'm sorry that Rita, who I don't doubt really was the sweet young person you remember, or if I do doubt it I'm not going to say so, has been so damaged by that experience that she is now prepared to kill people for it. And I'm sorry that you're so blinded by your memories of someone who may never have become your sweetheart that you don't even notice other women who might have an interest in your affections. Like the one sitting next to you right now.'

He was staring at her. 'What was that last bit?'

She opened her tablet and called up the list of addresses where they were supposed to check the owner of the Renault. 'Just drive, Jamie. First up is 22, Northumberland Close.'

***

It was the seventh Renault on the list. They didn't drive there immediately after leaving the house where the sixth was registered, because when Theresa read out the seventh address, Jamie looked as though he'd been hit with a lump hammer. He took a card out of his pocket. 'Read that address again.' When she did, he said, 'That's where the reunion is.'

Relief took hold of Theresa. Now she could tell him what she'd found out. She said, 'That isn't Bill Tulley's address, Jamie.'

'He didn't say it was his place. He just said

that's where the reunion was being held.'

'Did he say whether he'd had a good flight? Or how long he'd be staying here?'

'What?'

'Jamie. This reunion sounded very dodgy to me when you told me about it. So I went up to school and talked to the secretary there. Bill Tulley lives in Australia.'

'Oh. Well, maybe that's why he…'

'Jamie. The secretary gave me the names of people who were close to Bill Tulley at school. I went to see them.' She read them off her tablet. 'Does that sound like the people he would want to see if he held a reunion?'

'Well… Yes. Yes, I'm sure he would. They'd be first on his list.'

'None of them is invited. None of them has heard about a reunion. None of them is aware that Bill Tulley has come back from Australia. And all of them think, if he had, he'd have contacted them.'

Jamie was looking stunned. 'So… What…'

'Jamie. There is no reunion. So what you need to ask yourself is: why have you been invited to go tomorrow to a house at which is registered a dark blue Renault that may belong to a killer?'

'Theresa. Why did you go to all that trouble to check out Bill Tulley and his friends?'

'Were you listening when I mentioned people who might have an interest in your affections? Do you think someone that applies to would just sit back and take no notice when she thought you might be putting yourself in harm's way?' There could be no better time than this. She leaned over and kissed him on the cheek. 'You're going to have to face it, Jamie. There's only one reason you would have been invited to visit that house. You're next on the list. The woman you've yearned for all these years is going to kill you.'

'She blames me.'

'Don't look so grief stricken. Accept it. Rita Taylor isn't right in the head. Maybe it's down to what happened twenty years ago, maybe it's something more recent, maybe she's always been like that, but Rita is nuts. And the court will see that, and she'll be dealt with with compassion. But she will be taken off the streets, which is what she needs and what the rest of us need, for her protection and for ours. And we have to make that happen by calling MCIT.'

'No!'

'Yes! You're a policeman, Jamie. You're a policeman before you're anything. You do what all your training tells you to do.'

Jamie started the car and drove away from the curb. When Theresa clicked on the microphone, he said, 'Put that down.'

'Jamie, we don't have any choice.'

'I know that. We'll turn her in. But before we do, I want to see her. I want to tell her I'm sorry. To say I understand.'

Indecision was a new feeling for Theresa.

Usually, she knew what she ought to do and she did it. But this was Jamie. As if he understood what was in her mind, he said, 'You said you had feelings for me. If that's true, let me do it my way.'

'That's emotional blackmail.'

When they reached the street, Jamie parked a little way from the address. He said, 'Stay in the car.'

'Jamie, this is foolishness. You're dealing with killers.'

'I won't do anything stupid. But I don't want her to have the harshness of a police car driving up to the door. Please. Stay in the car.'

She watched as he walked away, turning through a gate a little distance from the car. She couldn't remember ever feeling so nervous. This must be what it was like watching your child going to school for the first day. You would feel like this because you loved your child so much. However much she had tried to deny it, that was the strength of her feelings for Jamie. This wooing wasn't some game that she would tire of playing. This was her whole life. And, when he walked through that gate, her whole life was what he was risking.

**

Deborah had seen the policeman walk through the gate and approach the front door. With a little frisson, she realised that this would not be just any copper – she knew who this must be. She said to Rita, who knew they had a caller but hadn't seen him, 'Nip upstairs and make sure Bernie Spence stays quiet.' When Rita had gone, Deborah went to the door.

When the cop gave his name, she felt a surge of elation as she realised that she'd been right. This wasn't the time she had planned – she'd intended Jamie Pearson to make his trip into the next world tomorrow, while Rita was away, and to get rid of the body before Rita came home – but fate was fate and you played the cards as they were dealt you. And he'd come alone! That meant the fates were on Deborah's side. They wanted her to succeed. Her excitement was such that she had to concentrate on what he was asking. 'Yes,' she said. 'Yes, we do have a dark blue Renault. It's in a garage at the end of the back garden – we are between two roads here. Would you like to see it?'

'I don't need to,' said Jamie. 'I just need to confirm that it's here.' He held up the picture of Rita as the software suggested she would now be. 'Have you ever seen this woman?'

Deborah took the picture from his hands and looked at it with great care. She felt a strange affection for this man who was delivering himself into her hands. Her hands and Rita's, she reminded herself – Rita might think now that she didn't hold Jamie Pearson responsible for what had happened to her, but Deborah would bring her to see things as they really were. Deborah could always get Rita to see things the way Deborah saw them. She said, 'No, I'm sorry. I don't believe I've ever seen her before.' When Jamie looked disappointed, as though she had somehow failed him, she said, 'I have a lodger. She may have seen her – you can ask her if you like. But you'll have to go upstairs to do it – she's an artist and she hates being interrupted. Her studio is on the top floor.' She stood back, inviting Jamie in. He looked as though he was thinking about the wisdom of this, and she fixed him with her most innocent look. 'I need to be doing something in the kitchen, so if you'll excuse me…'

And she closed the front door and turned away, and after a few moments she heard rather than saw Jamie begin to mount the stairs.

***

Jamie knew he was making a mistake. He'd seen the look on Deborah's face when she said she didn't recognise the picture of Rita. He knew what that look meant. The police are lied to throughout their careers, and they can tell when it's happening. If this hadn't been Rita…

But it was Rita. And there she was, after all these years, sitting on the floor beside a woman who was tied to a chair with cable ties. The woman had obviously been trying to free herself, because the chair had fallen on its side. He didn't know how long she'd been in that position, but her distress was clear.

Rita was stroking the woman's hair, and talking to her. In fact, crooning to her would be a more accurate description. 'You've got to last a bit longer, Bernadette. Deborah says we can't release you till the day after tomorrow.'

'For God's sake,' the woman sobbed. 'What kind of animals are you? Cut me free, for pity's sake.'

'Ah, darling, we can't do that. You know too much. But we'll make it nice for you when you go. If you know anything about the cases so far, you'll know we've masturbated the men as they died. Well, I've masturbated them. It wasn't something Deborah would have liked to do. But Deborah might be willing to masturbate you, Bernadette.' She put her hand on the reporter's ankle and slid it up her leg under her skirt. 'Will you like that? Will you like it if one of us gives you a wank while the other sends you into the darkness?' She giggled. 'That's a Deborah word, wank. I don't think she likes me using it.'

Theresa had been right. The sweet young girl he'd dreamed about was batshit crazy. He couldn't listen to this any more. He stepped forward. 'Move back, Rita. I'm going to free your prisoner.'

And then he was writhing on the floor, as Deborah put down her taser and began to haul him towards the chair Bernadette was tied to, so that she could tie him to the other side. When that was done, she took two full vials of morphine out of the fridge and put them on the windowsill. 'We may have to speed things up, Rita. Send them both on their way today. One full shot each.'

266

'No!' cried Rita. She left Bernadette and hugged Jamie to her. 'Not Jamie. Not now that he's found me at last.'

'What do you think he's going to do, woman? Settle down in a threesome? He's a cop. He'll turn us in. You want to spend the rest of your life in prison? Because I'm not prepared to do that.'

Now the crooning had started again, and this time it was aimed at him. She had her arms wrapped around his shoulders and she was almost singing the words to him. 'Oh, Jamie, Jamie, why did you have to come here? Why couldn't you have minded your own business?'

Still groggy from the taser hit, Jamie knew he had to reason with her. But how do you reason with someone who isn't sane? Who has never grown up, a woman's body containing a mind that had stopped developing when she was sixteen? And where was the other woman? The one who'd blasted him with a taser? She'd been there seconds ago, and now she was gone, disappeared without a word. Had Rita noticed? He didn't think she had.

***

Standing close to the window, but making sure she couldn't be seen from outside, Deborah had been aware of movement. Someone was just beyond the gate, peering round the hedge and surveying the house while trying to be invisible. The someone was female and wearing a police uniform. Deborah knew without even having to think about it that the gig was up. Jamie Pearson had not come alone. He had backup. And if there was one, others would be close behind. That was how those bastards worked. You only had to fall foul of them once to know that.

She slipped out of the room, down a flight of stairs, opened the locked cupboard and extracted her flight bag. She peeked once more from the window; the policewoman was speaking into a mobile phone. Time was running out. Back up the stairs, much faster this time. 'Rita! We have to go – now! Your copper is not alone. Now, Rita. Or I'll go without you.'

Rita was staring at her with that empty, vacuous look she sometimes adopted. Deborah had wondered from time to time just how genuine that look was – there were times when Rita seemed away with the fairies and times you felt she was all there. Rita said, 'What about Jamie?' And then she angled her head towards Bernadette Spence. 'What about her?'

'Leave them. They got lucky – we haven't got time to finish the job.'

Rita turned the full weight of her gaze on Jamie. 'You heard that? Deborah isn't going to kill you. And you know what? I was never going to let her. It's the one thing we disagreed on.' She giggled and pressed her lips to Jamie's forehead. 'I think she was jealous. Jealous of what you mean to me.'

Deborah said, 'Rita. We haven't got time for this. If you don't want to be caught, come with me,

268

but you have to do it now because I'm not staying any longer.' She looked at the face in front of her. Was this really the woman she'd loved? The one she'd been so close to for so long? Opened herself to as never before? Rita looked like a stranger. Any moment now, they were going to hear the thud of that big red battering ram the police used to break down doors that were locked against them. And when that happened it would be too late, because the police would be downstairs and the escape route was downstairs and Deborah would still be up here.

She wasn't thinking now about Rita. She was thinking about Mavis Ritzig, and how she'd ruled the tier Deborah's cell had been on, and what she'd done while her lieutenants pinned Deborah down. No-one was going to do that to Deborah again. She said, 'Last chance, Rita. If you're not coming, stay – but I'm out of here.' One more second to judge the effect of the threat and then she was running downstairs, backpack in her hand. She stopped once more, to grab three framed drawings, and then she picked up her keys and she was through the back door, locking it behind her. Up the garden path, through the gate which she also locked although she knew with a sinking heart that she was consigning Rita to the likes of Mavis Ritzig, and then she was checking that the folding bike was in the boot and the car was out of the garage and she was gone, keeping just under the speed limit. The stupidest thing in the world now would be to be stopped for speeding.

**

Jamie's relief when Deborah vanished was intense. He couldn't bring himself to believe that Rita, however crazy she obviously was, was capable of killing him. But the other one... He said, 'It's over, Rita. I'll make sure you're dealt with kindly, but it's finished. Cut us free.'

Rita snuggled closer to him. 'Not yet, Jamie. I like having you where you are.' She nuzzled his ear. 'Have you any idea how long I've wanted to do this? You know what I've done, Jamie. Don't you? Terence Carpenter? Michael Saville? Howard Diller? You know about them?'

'Yes, Rita, I know about them.'

'And you know it was me? Me and Deborah?'

'Yes, Rita, I know it was you. We know it was you.'

'They'll send me to jail, won't they? Except that it won't be jail, will it? It'll be one of those special hospitals. The ones for mad people. They'll say I'm nuts. Crazy. A mad woman. Do you think I'm crazy, Jamie?'

He looked at her, unwilling to answer, aware that he had never met anyone remotely as mad and conscious that she could do him a great deal of harm if she turned against him now.

'Will Jamie wait for Rita when they put her away?' She kissed him, a long, lingering kiss on the lips and he heard with relief the crash

270

downstairs as the big red key forced the door open. Then people were racing upstairs and the loudest voice suggested Theresa McErlane was leading the charge. Rita said, 'No, Jamie won't wait for Rita. Because they'll never let Rita out. Will they? They'll say she's too mad ever to be set free.' She picked up the two vials of morphine from where Deborah had left them. 'There's enough morphine in each of these to kill a person stone dead in less than two minutes. One is for her behind you, but we haven't got time for that. And the other one, my sweet Jamie, is for you.' She sat a little away from him and broke the first vial open. 'We can both go, Jamie. Together at last. For ever.' She pinched Jamie's nose closed. As Theresa and her backup cavalry charged through the door, Rita waved the morphine over Jamie's now open mouth. 'You let me down, Jamie. You should have protected me, and you didn't.'

'I know, Rita. And I'll never be able to tell you how sorry I am.'

There were tears in her eyes. 'Michael Saville said that. He told me how sorry he was.'

And she had killed him. But then she put the morphine to her own lips and swallowed the entire charge. She wrapped her arms around him. 'Don't forget me, Jamie. Let me hold you while I go.'

CHAPTER 28

The mood in the incident room was sombre. DCI Blazeley said, 'We had two killers. One is dead and one has vanished – escaped, when we were right on top of her. There's nothing to be done about Rita Taylor. She committed suicide rather than face arrest and trial, and that's what we will tell the coroner and IOPC. As for the woman calling herself Deborah Walsh who we now know to have been Sadie McIntosh, we have no idea where she is. And although we have her prints and her DNA, we don't know what she looks like, which doesn't help find her. Rayyan, what have you found out?'

'She left the crime scene in the dark blue Renault. That has now been found at Telford Services on the M54, apparently abandoned. Telford is a long way from Batterton but the service station has the advantage for someone on the run of not being actually on the motorway, so it gives escape options a motorway doesn't have. McIntosh's fingerprints were all over the car and on various items inside it including three empty picture frames. CCTV at the services captured a woman riding away from the car park on a fold-up bike. The image is nothing like clear enough to print. A similar bike was later found at the bus station and we've confirmed the presence of McIntosh's fingerprints on it, but no bus driver remembers a passenger who might have been her.'

Susanna said, 'And the bus station may have been a red herring. She may have been making for the train station. Or even hitching a lift.'

'She may,' said Rayyan, 'and we've been in touch with the station manager, but no likely candidate turns up on CCTV either approaching the station or on any of the platforms. As the DCI said, the main problem is we don't know what she looks like. There's the mug shot taken when Sadie McIntosh was arrested, but that was a long time ago and…Well, it was a mug shot. We can try to update it but we won't get anything good enough for people to identify her. We've also checked car rental companies. No-one rented a car to anyone called Deborah Walsh or Sadie McIntosh.'

Blazeley said, 'We don't even know she's travelling under either of those names. Marion, who was checking out people Sadie McIntosh might have met in prison?'

Nicola held up her hand. 'That was me, guv. There's one very obvious candidate. Adrianna Radovic was serving five years for forgery. She lives in Grimsby. I got Humberside Police to invite her for a voluntary interview. She told them to go to hell. The DI I spoke to said he'd already spoken to his custody sergeant and the custody sergeant said, if they tried to bring her in against her will on what we have now, she'd refuse to accept her.'

'I can't say I blame her,' said Blazeley. All right. We don't know what she's calling herself, we don't know where she is, and we don't know what she looks like. What do we know about her?'

Rayyan said, 'That house isn't really hers. It belonged to an artist called Dorothea Tate. Dorothea Tate died. She was seventy-two. Deborah Walsh was nursing her at home at the time.'

'Cause of death?' asked Blazeley.

'Natural causes, according to the doctor who signed it off.'

'A doctor who presumably didn't know what Sadie McIntosh had got up to as a nurse before she became Deborah Walsh.'

'Yes, sir. But the thing is, Deborah Walsh has been living in that house ever since. Rent free. Dorothea Tate left no relatives, or none that were ever found. Deborah Walsh changed the council tax and utilities bills into her name. She also somehow managed to get the bank to give her a mortgage for ninety-five percent of the value of the house by persuading them that she was Dorothea Tate. I've included the original documents on the warrant so we can see how she pulled that off. According to the bank, it will take some time to produce them – they are stored somewhere else and the manager has no idea where.'

'There must have been an account in Dorothea Tate's name, then?'

'There was. And it's been emptied – bit by bit over a period of time and in cash. So there is no possibility of tracing where it went.'

Blazeley threw up his hands in what looked like despair. 'Well, until we get a handle on where Sadie McIntosh is now, there's not much we can do. And she clearly isn't short of money, so she may not even still be in the country. How is Jamie Pearson making out?'

Theresa, who had been invited to attend this briefing having witnessed the endgame, put up a hand. 'They took him to hospital, sir. I had to force him to go because he really didn't want to, but he'd had a nasty shock. Really, sir, I think he should be forced to take leave. You know what he's like... Well, you don't know what he's like, sir, but I do... He'll want to come straight back to work and he really isn't up to it.'

'All right. Susanna, speak to his sergeant and get that done. What about the reporter, Theresa – did she go to hospital too?'

'Not a bit of it, sir. Even though she'd been held there longer than Jamie. When I said we were taking her to hospital for a checkup, she said, not on your life. She said she was going nowhere until she filed her story. She rang her editor and he sent a car for her.'

'No doubt we'll be reading that story very shortly. As if we didn't have enough to worry about.'

Susanna said, 'There's something we're missing here, sir. Theresa. How did you know there was something wrong about that place?

Because, if you hadn't called for help when you did, we'd almost certainly have lost a constable.'

And so Theresa ran through the story of her suspicions about the reunion Jamie had been invited to, and how she'd used her day off to check, first with the school and then with individuals who should have been invited, and satisfied herself that there was to be no reunion and that Jamie had been invited for other reasons altogether. She was conscious as she spoke that the story she told was meeting with approval. But all Blazeley said when it was over was, 'You did well, Theresa. Well done. Right, the rest of you; we may not get a lead on Sadie McIntosh for some time. If the worst happens, we may never get one. SOCO are going to be in that house for at least a month. If they turn up anything worth following, we'll follow it. Until then, I'm sure you all have lots of things to do that are completely unconnected with the series of murders we've been dealing with. Go and do them.'

***

Things unwound themselves, more easily for some than for others. Ralph Townsend was charged with the rape of an underage girl. In view of the length of time that had elapsed and the successful and blameless life he had led since then, he was sentenced to four years imprisonment. The *Post* made a front-page splash of the story, Townsend's children were ridiculed at school, the board of the company where he had made a huge success as Sales and Marketing Director told him there would be no job to return to when he got out and his wife filed for divorce.

When it became clear that Rigby Hewitt was not going to come back to Britain to give evidence, Bazza Humphreys hoped that the case against him would be abandoned. He was not so lucky. He had made a full confession in which both what he said and how he looked when he said it were recorded. The CPS agreed there was a case to answer, and Bazza was charged, pleaded guilty, and was sentenced to two years. As he'd already spent more than a year remanded in custody, he was released immediately after the trial. When Ralph Townsend complained to his lawyer that his sentence had been twice as long as Bazza's, his lawyer pointed out the fundamental difference that Bazza's "victim" had been a willing participant, while Ralph's had never stopped begging to be spared. The Post Office refused to take Bazza back, but he found work as a van driver which, because he was required to interact with fewer people, made him happier than he had been before.

As for Rigby Hewitt himself, his attempts to ignore what was happening in court in the country where he had once lived proved fruitless. Bernadette Spence found out where he was and sold the story to a North American magazine with a huge circulation famous for publishing trashy stories about celebrities. But Rigby's fears for his career proved unfounded – his agent found that the demand for the actor's work had never been so heavy.

Susanna spent what she thought a shocking amount of money on a hairdresser. The wedding she had faced with trepidation was a great success. Towards the end of the day, Maria, the sister of Chris McAvoy's late wife, took her to one side. 'Thanks for coming, Susanna. And I want you to know, all of us think Chris could not have made a better choice.' She squeezed Susanna's hand, and Susanna thought for a moment that she was going to burst into tears.

As Jamie Pearson's sick leave drew to an end, Theresa McErlane visited him at home as often as her new duties allowed. He said, 'You made it, then. You're a DC now?'

'They know I've passed my sergeant's exams, but they said they didn't have room on the headcount for a DS – only a DC. I don't believe any of that – I don't think I'll be promoted until I've proved myself.'

'That won't take you long.'

Watching him, Theresa could tell that the burden he'd carried for so long was growing lighter. He was leaving the past behind. One evening, she brought with her a travelling bag from which she took a nightie that she tucked under a pillow on Jamie's bed, underwear that she put into a drawer and skirts and tops that went into a wardrobe. 'We need more storage space.'

Jamie said, 'Am I allowed to ask what's going on?'

'Of course you are. We are practising. For when we get married. So we are perfect at it when it happens.'

'We're getting married?'

'I thought next spring. That all right with you? You'll find I don't make many demands, but I do make one. There will be two wedding rings – one for me in the usual way, and one for you. Just to make sure that any woman who looks at you realises they left it too late. You're taken.'

Nicola's sister, Sasha, told her, 'You're going to have to meet this George Clooney lookalike, because if I don't make that happen Mummy is not going to forgive me. It doesn't have to lead to anything, but you do have to do it.' And Nicola did do it, and it didn't lead to anything, and her mother continued to grumble about the daughter who insisted on doing a job that should be left to men while failing to fulfil a daughter's duty to provide her mother with grandchildren.

And Nicola continued to take no notice.

POSTSCRIPT
18 MONTHS LATER

Bill Blazeley received a phone call from Police Scotland. He called Susanna David to his office. 'Sadie McIntosh's fingerprints have shown up. She got into a fight with a woman called Mavis Ritzig – an ex-con, apparently. She's in a police station in Dunfermline under the name Ellie Driver, and they can only hold her on what they've got for another twenty-four hours. Get someone up there without delay to arrest her and bring her down here.'

DCs Theresa Pearson and Nicola Hayward were dispatched to Dunfermline. They arrived to find a police station in chaos. 'I don't know what to tell you,' said a crestfallen custody sergeant. 'I don't know how it happened.'

'It isn't your fault,' said Nicola. 'You weren't to know she was a suicide risk.' And there'll be hell to pay, she thought, if someone connects this suicide with Rita's and realises that Batterton didn't warn you.

'I hope the fiscal takes the same view.'

Nicola said, 'This is going to be one of those things that haunt you forever. Why? Why did she kill herself?'

'She knew she was going to prison,' said Theresa. 'She'd been there before. She knew what to expect. The only way to know why she couldn't face being there again would be to find out what happened the first time.'

'As it happens,' said the custody sergeant, 'there's someone who may be able to help with that. Mavis Ritzig. She did time with Ellie Driver when Ellie Driver was Sadie McIntosh. The other nurses at the hospital say Ellie Driver was a bit reserved but the nicest person you could ever hope to meet – but then Mavis Ritzig was taken into A&E with alcohol poisoning and according to those who were there Ellie Driver simply went berserk.'

But when they asked Mavis Ritzig what had happened to cause bad blood between her and Sadie McIntosh, Mavis invited them to perform on themselves an act everyone knew to be biologically impossible.

A search of Ellie Driver's flat didn't produce much, but it did turn up three drawings of Deborah Walsh, beautifully executed and signed by Rita Taylor. Nicola said, 'That explains the three empty frames. If we'd had these, we'd have caught her long ago. No wonder she took them with her.'

FROM THE AUTHOR

I hope you enjoyed this. If you did, you may like to know that *Death to Order*, the second book in the *Batterton Police Series*, will be published on 1 February, 2022. Here's how it starts:

Jensen Bartholomew, well fed and self-satisfied, was Zooming with his brother, Cedric who looked as though he hadn't eaten a full meal in a long time when the door behind him opened and a figure entered covered head to foot in a black gown and wearing a Guy Fawkes mask. As Jensen watched, the figure wrapped something around Cedric's neck and pulled it tight. Cedric half rose from his chair. His hands struggled to free himself and his feet stamped a furious tattoo on the worn lino beneath them, but the figure did not relent. Cedric sank out of sight. The figure leaned in close to the screen and pointed through it at Jensen. In a deep and gravelly voice, it said, 'You're next.' Then the screen went as dead as Cedric.

Want something else to read? On the next page you'll find my books written under other names.

Sharon Wright: Butterfly *by John Lynch*
No-one gives Sharon a chance – except Sharon
A crime novel set in gritty, grimy South London and rural France.

Darkness Comes *by John Lynch*
Ted Bailey stares Death in the face. And Death blinks first
Ted Bailey has got away with drug dealing, gunrunning, and even murder. Now he faces the ultimate judge. But all is not as it seems.

The Making of Billy McErlane *by John Lynch*
Born into the family from hell. Destined for a life of crime. In prison at 14. But Billy's life is not over yet
Begins in tragedy and ends in hope. A bittersweet story of love, loss and refusal to accept what life offers.

The James Blakiston Series *by R J Lynch*
A Just and Upright Man and *Poor Law* (with more to come)
Set in the north-east of England in the 1760s, historical fiction from the point of view of people at the bottom of the social heap and not the top.

Printed in Great Britain
by Amazon

21810662R00166